PRAISE FOR *THE GARDEN*

'With an impressive atmosphere of Conradian disquiet, this is a vivid and exceptionally exciting novel.'

—Sebastian Barry

'A prodigiously gifted writer.'

—Fred D'Aguiar

'A lush, tough evocation of obsession and betrayal, this is noir with a poet's touch. *The Garden* is a book about beauty, blood, heat and ruin. A rich and satisfying read.'

—Anne Enright

'Luminous as a bruise, vividly compelling, oozing shades of Hemingway in its depiction of lost souls stalking salvation in a damaged, defiant Eden.'

—Mia Gallagher

'Intense and riveting. *The Garden* has a savage beauty that haunts.'

—Danielle McLaughlin

'*The Garden* is a bitter but beautiful pill, an American novel that somehow only a world-class Irish poet could have written.'

—Christian Nagle, author of *Flightbook*

'Paul Perry has written a highly intelligent novel in which the pursuit of true beauty can only cause pain. Beckettian in its themes and yet lavish in its descriptions, this Garden is far from Eden.'

—Liz Nugent

'A gripping novel of disorder and desire, evoking superbly a humid, claustrophobic world in precise, headlong prose. Read it.'

—Kevin Power

At once a mystery and a meditation on landscape, The Garden is Paul Perry's most gorgeous novel to date.

—Michelle Richmond,
New York Times Best Selling Author of *The Marriage Pact*

THE
GARDEN

PAUL
PERRY

NEW ISLAND

THE GARDEN
First published in 2021 by
New Island Books
Glenshesk House
10 Richview Office Park
Clonskeagh
Dublin D14 V8C4
Republic of Ireland
www.newisland.ie

Hardback ISBN: 978-1-84840-799-2
eBook ISBN: 978-1-84840-800-5

British Library Cataloguing in Publication Data. A CIP catalogue record for this book
is available from the British Library.

Typeset by JVR Creative India
Cover design by Luke Bird, lukebird.co.uk
Printed by ScandBook, scandbook.com

New Island received financial assistance from The Arts Council (An Chomhairle
Ealaíon), Dublin, Ireland.

New Island Books is a member of Publishing Ireland.

10 9 8 7 6 5 4 3 2 1

'I feel as if heaven lay close upon the earth and I between them both, breathing through the eye of a needle.'

Lawrence Durrell, *Justine*

'Because the world is so full of death and horror, I try again and again to console my heart and pick the flowers that grow in the midst of Hell.'

Hermann Hesse, *Narcissus and Goldmund*

When I first saw Romeo, I thought, *here comes trouble.* I was outside the house, smoking. The sun was setting over the farm, the light dusky. He walked without purpose up the long gravel driveway, a worn green canvas carry-all slung over his back. He wore a pair of torn jeans and a white cotton shirt. He looked like he'd been walking a long time, as if he'd gotten lost, or taken an unwanted detour. His boots were dusty, his face sun-beaten. Even in his youth, there was a lassitude about him, a sense, as he approached, of confusion and weary disdain.

'Hello,' he said stepping from the shadows. His voice surprised me – there was none of the urgency I was expecting. Instead, there was pride, apathy and a familiar Latin inflection. 'You're the boss?'

'Not me,' I said.

I threw the butt of my cigarette to the ground and stubbed it out.

'I'm looking for the orchid keeper.'

'He's resting,' I said.

He swung his bag from his back and put it between his feet.

'I'll wait,' he said.

He looked about him – took in the house, the barracks, orchard, greenhouses, lab and sheds. He saw the workers bending to their business, cutting, sawing and hammering – a quiet hum of industrious activity all around.

'I'm Swallow,' I said.

He held out his hand.

'Romeo,' he grinned, then shook my hand strongly, and let it go.

So, this was Romeo. I'd been expecting something else. Blanchard had said he was bringing expertise to the Garden. Not a man on foot, looking as if his every belonging was in a bag by his feet. Not someone so young. His youth, it smacked of inexperience, and that's not what we needed.

After a time, I said, 'There's no sense in waiting here. I can show you your bunk.' I pointed to the barracks where our casual labour slept. He considered what I'd said. 'Give you a chance to rest before Blanchard wakes.'

He looked unsure. Regardless, I walked towards the barracks. Eventually, he followed.

'He likes a siesta?' Romeo asked dourly. 'The boss?'

'He's in a blue funk,' I replied.

He looked behind him down the path he'd just trodden – the sun dropping farther, the sky spoiling. There was something regretful in his gaze, his eyes dark and downcast. Half a dozen of the workers passed us and bid us good evening. Romeo kept quiet, and close.

We went into the barracks – a harsh-sounding structure – but it wasn't. It was simply what we called it. A glorified shed, it had hot water, showers, a small kitchen and a host of bunks. Granted, it had taken a hammering, but it was repaired now, mostly, though it creaked and sang in the wind. I'd somehow got used to it.

I showed the new man the spare bunk at the back, and he threw his bag onto the mattress. The other beds were covered with clothes; boots and sneakers lined each one beneath. The set-up was like something a sorry battalion of lost soldiers may have endured, all discipline gone. Still, it was not quite the dosshouse it might have been. We had our rules.

Romeo gazed up toward the skylight and then to the back door, which was open, offering a frame to the wire fencing that enclosed the farm. A gentle breeze blew through the building, welcoming in the maw of humidity.

'The john is through that door,' I said, pointing. 'Showers too. You can do your laundry come Sunday.'

'Laundry?' he said suspiciously.

I shrugged. At this stage, I didn't know what Romeo did or did not need to know. I'd no idea how long he would even be here. Granted, you could say that about any of the workers who came and went. Mostly folk picked up whatever it was they needed to know throughout the working day by talking to one another. But what Romeo wanted to know, and what he needed to know, was not clear to me.

Some of the workers had left before the hurricane had hit, but there had always been a steady flow of more of them to take their place. Blanchard had called me to the office and asked me to make room for the new guy. This meant vacating one of the beds in the barracks – not a problem – but I never liked to let a good man go, even if Blanchard was having difficulty paying them all.

So, I released Chaves, a young Argentinian worker with a wife and child living elsewhere. He was doleful but didn't dispute the dismissal. And as the days neared to Romeo's arrival, I'd sensed a certain curiosity in me grow, something I'd not anticipated – a change, an excitement even, strange though it felt.

I tried to imagine what this new man made of the place. He looked like he'd seen and survived worse. And with the muted swagger about him, I sensed too that he'd also experienced something more magnificent, something more excessive. As if there was a touch of the gambler about him. Still, he hadn't seen the extent of the damage.

'Show me around?' he asked, eyeing his bag.

'It'll be safe,' I said, as if to reassure him. I could have told him how when there last was a dispute here, it had ended in blood, a pool of it not far from his bunk. I could have told him how the wronged party had cornered the man, and how Blanchard and I had walked away while justice was meted out. The smell of bleach only served to remind us of the cost of committing a crime here, in the Garden, as Blanchard called the nursery and grounds around us; as if it had some Edenic quality to it. Maybe it had, once upon a time.

Blanchard had bought the land only ten years previous, when it was nothing but wasteland. Slowly, he'd flattened the terrain, paved the road access, and introduced electricity and water. Now it amounted to sixty acres of outdoor and indoor growing.

We were far enough from the highway, behind full tree coverage, and secured by perimeter fences for privacy. Surrounded by wooded acreage with no neighbours to speak of, there were five saw-tooth grow houses, a glaze-roofed mist house and a number of shade-houses. The Garden had been a haven for growing and selling orchids – that is, until the hurricane hit.

We walked out into the dusk. Around us, the sounds of Spanish faded. About the perimeter of the grounds, I pointed out the various repairs which required attention. Swathes of fencing had been torn down. The fig and orange trees of the fruit orchard were bent or breaking; large branches lay snapped on the ground, waiting to be removed. Two banana trees were shredded. Shade-cloth was in ribbons. The bamboo was stripped, pots smashed and a trailer remained on its side. The violence of the hurricane was apparent everywhere you looked.

'It's worse than I thought,' Romeo said.

The fields were mostly drained, but there was still a faint sucking sound with each step we took.

'If you've come for hurricane repairs, you're late.'

I meant it as a joke, but Romeo didn't laugh. He kicked at the wheel of a backhoe. I showed him the boilers and the back-up generator, crucial during hurricane season, and the heaters, fans, the temperature and irrigation controls. Then there was the metal building with the loading dock, and of course the greenhouses.

'There's a lot left to do,' he said.

He was right, and the enormity of the work remaining depressed me. Together with the thought that another man was not going to make much difference, no matter what his expertise was. Unless, of course, Blanchard's plan came off.

'But that's not all I'm here to do, no?'

I shook my head. I wasn't sure how much he thought I knew about his appearance or how much I should let on I knew. Blanchard could be evasive at the best of times. I'd learned not to ask too many questions. We all had. So, I didn't know what to tell Romeo. For months, Blanchard had been blighted by stress and anxiety at losing most of our orchid stock. There was talk of debt and insolvency, and though he was a man of many ideas, his obsession was orchids. And after the hurricane he decided we needed to do something radical. What he wanted was the ghost orchid. That, he reasoned, would make everything right. The unattainable, the magical, a flower which by its very existence suggested there was no death, that time did not somehow unravel like a stitch of cloth thrown into a ravine.

'Were you here when it hit?'

'Yeah,' I said, 'I was here.'

The hurricane that came through the Garden had gained momentum over the Gulf, and when it landed it had almost destroyed the place. I told Romeo how it had pummelled us, how the barracks' roof had been torn off.

I told him the main house itself had been shuttered. Its windows had barely remained intact, but its side and panelling were pounded and needed attention. The greenhouses had been levelled, but had been mostly rebuilt.

'The sound of the wind was like gunfire,' I said.

I'm not sure Romeo wanted to know any of this. I think maybe he was looking for a way in, a story, something personal maybe. So I told him how the men and I had watched the news on the TV Blanchard had installed in the barracks. Some of the men had decided the Garden was not a safe place to be, and had left. Who knows where they went? North to Georgia, or home, wherever that was. We never saw them again. That's how it goes. Others had nowhere to go. They stayed. Some didn't believe the warnings, or they didn't care, and kept about the storm protection work we gave them.

We went on hurricane watch. Not long after, evacuations became mandatory.

'You'll stay,' Blanchard had said.

I'd nowhere else to go, so I said, 'Sure. I'll stay.'

I guess Blanchard appreciated that.

We went to work and tried desperately to secure the Garden's buildings. I was trying to give Romeo a sense of what it was like, so I said, 'Once I was in a thunderstorm.'

'Oh yeah?' he said.

'I was flying from Chicago with a friend. And we were struck by lightning.'

'No?'

'People shot out of their seats. The plane stalled, then dropped.'

'You thought you were going to die?'

'Pretty much.'

'And?'

'And the hurricane … it was worse.'

I told him that when it landed, the remaining men and I had hunkered down in the main house and listened to one of them, Miguel, pray.

He'd been high as a kite, and I said, 'I watched him walk out into the storm and let the rain wash over him like he was some kind of a lunatic preacher.'

Romeo closed his eyes as if he were imagining the scene. I didn't say Miguel was lucky not to have been swept away by the winds or to have been hit by lightning. Romeo had already seen the mess. He could figure the rest out for himself.

'Welcome to paradise,' I said. It was something we said to every new recruit. Blanchard had said it to me. I was aware that to say it now, it sounded ironic, cruel even. There was a hint of irritation in my voice. I don't know why. Where were you? I thought. How could you not have known the hurricane was bad?

I said, 'Afterwards, there were nights when we slept beneath the stars.'

Romeo asked me where I was from. I told him Ireland. He looked at me from the corner of his eye – taking me in. Then we made our way through the grounds and talked some more. 'Your English is good,' I said to him. He said he'd learned a lot of English when he'd gone to Belize to study. He didn't say what, or where from, and he gave me the impression that he didn't want me to ask. As the sun sank beyond the horizon we returned to the office.

'When can I see him?' Romeo said then.

Darkness was falling. You could hear the ticking of cicadas from the gloom about us.

'Tomorrow,' I said.

He was disappointed.

'You said he was taking a nap.'

'He was, but the jeep is gone now.'

That should have been enough of an explanation, but not for Romeo.

'I need to speak to him. To tell him I am here.'

I shook my head. 'It looks like he went to eat with his wife, Meribel.'

'I need to discuss the details of my employment.'

For some reason, I thought what he'd last said was funny, and I began to laugh a little. This only made him mad. The purposeless gait up the driveway had given way to an urgency, and, if I'm not mistaken, a desperation. Still, I knew not to call Blanchard, not even with the arrival of the new man. He was protective of his time with Meribel.

'Tomorrow,' I said.

We walked back to the barracks, and he sat on the edge of his bunk. The others eyed him warily, but he ignored them. He remained resigned. He may even have been exhausted. He unzipped his bag and surveyed his meagre belongings – the usual: toothbrush, a pack of smokes, and some clothes, a maroon hoodie, a pair of jeans, socks and briefs.

For a split second, I felt like he was a kindred spirit of sorts, or that at one time, I *was* him – arriving somewhat hopefully to the Garden, walking up the gravel path with nothing to my name, no country and few belongings – only to be disappointed, as if I'd come to a dead end. He was undocumented, I imagined, much like I was, one of the lost, of a legion where the endless highways of traffic, the desolate drinking holes, the daytime neon and violent pulse of sunlight, the ever-unpredictable wash of sleepless nights and the memory of what had been, and the bitter broken pledge of what could have been beat through my blood on and on into each insomniac night.

He reached into his bag and pulled out a facecloth. 'There are always people like us.'

'Like us?'

'To clean up.' He smiled.

'The boss wants more than that.'

'He wants to be rich,' Romeo said, burying his face in the cloth. Now it was his turn to laugh, but his laughter was callow, and thin.

'Sure, but first – he needs to keep this place from going under,' I said.

Romeo wiped the day's grime and dried sweat from his face, and for some reason, I began to be wary of the wiry man before me. He sensed my recalcitrance and folded his cloth away. I could tell the other men had been listening. I paused and let the silence return. Eventually, the men filled it. They whispered to themselves about their families, about food and money.

Later that night, as I smoked outside, I heard the jeep return. The engine died, and the doors opened. There was the sound of voices. They were neither hushed nor raised. Blanchard was speaking in his curt, but polite fashion. Meribel, was listening patiently, replying with considerate humour. Their words wavered in the air. Then the jeep doors shut. They walked inside. From where I sat on the barracks' deck, through one greenhouse and another, I could see a light go on.

I imagined Blanchard going to the cabinet and pouring himself and his wife a drink. I imagined him lighting a cigar. Their house had been battered – shutters had been unhinged, windows smashed. The roof needed attention. After the lab, it had been the priority repair.

I heard Romeo stir. Here was another insomniac. Or, at least, the kind of person who slept with one eye open. He came out onto the deck. We didn't say anything to one another. He went to sit in the hammock. Back and forth he swung, blowing smoke into the night, watching the movements of Blanchard and his wife within the house.

After a time, I went back to bed. The tension in me disappeared. For weeks, I'd wondered who the new man would be, and now he was here. What I felt at that moment was something else. A kind of frustration. Something had shifted within the Garden – its energy had been displaced. I was no longer tense, but I wasn't easy either. I recognised a quiet thrumming in my blood: the new man reminded me of someone; he reminded me of my brother Jamie, or what he might have been like.

Outside, Romeo lit one cigarette after another, his lighter clicking open and shut, punctuating the nightfall. The men turned over in their sleep. My eyes grew heavy. Around me the mosquitos' buzzing rose and fell. And still the old hammock swung and squeaked. The next thing I knew, it was morning.

For the past few years, things had been much the same. Blanchard was the boss, with Meribel his wife, and sometimes assistant, by his side. There was the ageless Miguel, the Mexican, referred to sometimes by Blanchard as *my man Miguel*. And there was the barracks crew who, though not fixed as such, inhabited the barracks most months of the year. In fact, there had always been a steady flow of workers. Many stayed for a season, but few stayed much longer. There was no need, and no work for them during the low or off-season in any case. A few returned, but most were incarcerated, deported, or even killed for one reason or another. If they were lucky, they found work elsewhere. The only ones who stayed were stalwarts, all trusted, unquestioning workers.

After the hurricane, it was all about repairs, but there were cost implications, and Blanchard was not a generous man. Stock had been decimated. He discussed whether he could even afford storm-water management systems, and yet he was willing to take a risk on Romeo.

At first, I wondered what he could do that nobody else could. What was his special set of skills? When I said as much to Blanchard, he replied evenly, 'He's the kind of man we need.'

'What do you mean?' I asked.

'He has what it takes.'

These were clichés, and Blanchard knew it. He was not normally a man to indulge in hackneyed language, so when I persisted, he finally gave way. 'It's to do with our stock,' he said. 'I need something special in order to bounce back.'

It's true we had experienced losses. The insurance companies took months to reimburse if they ever did, and it rarely ever matched the actual value of what was lost. My first thought then about our new man was that he could do something Blanchard, Meribel or I could not – a specialist, in other words.

'The ghost?' I said to Blanchard. 'Is that what this is about?'

'Neither you nor I know how to breed it now, do we? So yes, Swallow, it is about the ghost.'

I didn't want to be involved with anything illegal. I hadn't renewed my permits to stay in the country, which was my own fault, a wariness I had with authority after the military, so it meant my life for some years now was under the radar and off the books. I didn't want to do anything which would jeopardise that vulnerable position. And yet, having worked here for years, I'd become bewitched by the ghost orchid, and often heard Blanchard talk of finding it deep in the Fakahatchee Strand, and when he discussed how 'the ghost' was something the Garden needed to survive, I began to feel I finally had a mission in life. The ghost gave me that; in many ways, it kept me at the Garden.

The next morning when I woke, Romeo was standing over me.

'Bring me to the boss,' he said.

It sounded like an order. But as an order, it was hard to take seriously. He was half-dressed, and his hair was wet. He looked more like a kid than the man who'd arrived the previous evening. Impatient, rather than eager.

It wasn't quite dawn. Outside, the dark was giving way to the morning sun. It was still weak, but would soon climb steadily. Even this late in the year, there was heat in its ascent, but not as much. It already felt like winter was on its way.

'Blanchard will be in here in good time,' I said.

'I need to see him,' Romeo replied impatiently.

I didn't know what to say to this. It wasn't the way we worked. Sure, Romeo was different to our other labour force, but for some reason I wanted him to wait. I carried on with my morning preparations: a cigarette on the deck, bitter black coffee.

Romeo seemed always to follow – with his eyes, if not with his person. He was ever watchful, ever wary. 'What am I to do?' he said in Spanish.

Most of the men's English was poor, and I'd picked up enough Spanish along the way to communicate with them, and between the languages we made ourselves understood. But there was no issue with Romeo.

'Maybe start by getting dressed.' I said. 'Then you can muck in.'

The barracks' crew were getting dressed – smoking, drinking coffee, talking. There was a quiet reverence to the routine. I sat up and pulled on my boots. Miguel approached. Without saying anything, he handed Romeo a mug of coffee. Romeo took it wordlessly, went back to his bunk and finished dressing.

'Those boots,' I called to him. 'They're no good for the fields.'

He looked down at the soft leather of his cowboy boots and shrugged.

'I didn't come here to work in the fields.'

'I'll find you something,' I said, and dug out a pair of steel-tipped work boots which I placed by the end of his bed. He looked at them briefly with amusement and ignored them.

'You're the new guy,' Miguel said.

Romeo sipped his coffee.

'What will you do here?'

Romeo was looking into his cup. I answered for him.

'He's working with us,' I said.

Of course, I knew the others would speculate. Why were we taking on a new man when we had to let others go? Where is the money coming from? But I also knew they wouldn't say anything. We worked together. We ate together. Sometimes we drank together. If one of the men were green, or homesick, or not right, they might share something of the past, or something personal. But it was a rare and unwise thing to do, in my experience. We kept to ourselves. It was safer like that.

'Come on,' I said to Romeo, and he followed, lighting a cigarette and squinting into the early-morning sunlight.

Miguel came too, but instead of walking next to us, the new man walked a little behind, as if he were shadowing me, literally looking over my shoulder.

I said, 'The first thing to do is check the sprinklers – then see which flowers need water, and what plants want fertiliser.'

Romeo nodded nonchalantly, but looked confused.

'I'm here for the ghost. Not this.'

'I know,' I said. 'But we don't have it.'

'You don't?'

'No, and until we do, you can help out, okay?'

Blanchard appeared at the shade-houses. A tall, lank man, he was cleaning his glasses with the end of a red bandana. The gesture covered for the formal, serious man he was. He took the brown flat-brimmed rancher from his head and swatted away the flies.

'You're here,' he said to Romeo.

'He arrived last night,' I said.

The two men shook hands.

'He told me not to disturb you,' Romeo said.

Blanchard nodded.

'How was your journey? Nothing too eventful, I hope?'

'No,' Romeo said dolefully.

'Good, good,' Blanchard said, pointing to the tangled shade-cloth which lay about us, black and shroud-like. 'As you can see, things are ... poorly. Not to put too fine a point on it, but we are struggling. Come. Let us show you around what we once called paradise, and which is now ... well, something else.'

He turned and beckoned us to follow him, and together we walked through the Garden, where the cordgrass was long and wet.

Blanchard turned to Romeo, 'But we're happy you're here, you know.' He put his arm about the man awkwardly, 'Very happy. We've been waiting for you.'

Romeo smiled.

'I'm looking forward to getting to work. To seeing the lab.'

Blanchard looked determined, earnest. 'Yes,' he said, 'the lab, of course.'

But we didn't go there. There was so much still left to do. Repairs were ongoing. I sometimes wondered if we'd ever get back to normal.

'Swallow,' Blanchard called. 'Break it down.'

I began with my morning update: number of men present, itinerary for the day's repairs, stock, outside jobs, figures, inventory, stuff like that. Blanchard wanted a detailed itinerary — he wanted it verbally, and he wanted it quick-fire. It was always a part of the morning which rattled me. What worried me that morning was that the temperatures in the greenhouses needed to be right, but the thermostats were old, and many of them were simply not working after the hurricane.

'We need new thermostats,' I said.

'Yes,' Blanchard said, but his tone wasn't reassuring. In fact, it was as if he wasn't listening to me at all, as if he was too distracted by the immensity of the task to really take in the detail of what needed to be done. So much so I was pretty sure I'd be saying the same thing about the thermostats again the following week.

'What about the ramp to the load house?' he asked.

With the barracks to our rear, three greenhouses stood before us, and behind it the lab. The ramp had been smashed, and it hadn't been repaired. Because we weren't expecting any deliveries, I didn't think it a priority.

Romeo stepped closer to me. As I struggled to answer Blanchard, it felt like the irascible impatience of Romeo had not dissipated. It felt like he was on the verge of saying something, of blurting out, at any moment, a sliver of pique which would unsettle everyone.

Blanchard waved his arm. 'Cut,' he said, meaning the grass.

The request was noted. Miguel beckoned two men from their chores in the fields, and when they came, he doled out instructions, and the men went about their business in silent obedience, machetes in hand.

Blanchard smiled and turned. He walked steadily towards the ostrich ferns and held a leaf in his hands. Gently, he massaged it between his finger and thumb, pulled at it and placed it into his mouth and chewed. Then his attention was drawn to one of the men who balanced a watering can over a potted orchid.

'One of the few survivors,' he said to Romeo.

Water flowed onto the flower's roots and dripped onto the table. The man mopped his brow. A good deal of order had been restored – the tables and protective structures were once again intact – but there was still a ways to go. The greenhouses had been mostly jerry-rigged, but a torn screen door, a stop sign and other wind-blown garbage still littered the fields about us. And yet there was a beauty to the scene – the sheer variety and vibrancy of plant-life seemed to dye my field of vision. You could almost feel the thickets breathe.

Romeo reached out and took the watering can from the man.

'Too much water,' he said. 'It's damaged.' He pointed to the bruised stem. 'See? It needs to dry out.' He handed the plant back, and Blanchard smiled before walking on with the rest of us finally in tow.

I oversaw the repairs, Blanchard called it 'the rehabilitation'. In my opinion, his stewardship of these efforts was suspect, lacked a certain and necessary application. I guess the financial strain he was undergoing was too much for him. For a variety of reasons, I'd wanted to take more control, but I'd either not been allowed, or hadn't made my interest and ability obvious enough. It'd bothered me, sure. I'd tried not to become resentful, and of course, it was my own inertia as much as anything else which annoyed me.

To add to that sense of discomfort, I also felt like I was part of a system of exploitation. Blanchard was white. I was white. While all the workers were immigrants, mostly Central and South Americans. When I said something to Blanchard about the balance of power, he'd paused. 'When did the Irish become white?' he said. I had nothing to answer this with, but the uneasy position I was in, as Blanchard's lieutenant, never left me.

'When are we going to talk business?' Romeo asked.

Blanchard stopped. He looked down at the man's cowboy boots and walked towards the sausage tree. The tree had always unnerved me with its strange-shaped fruit, but it was a favourite of Blanchard's, and it had survived the hurricane somehow.

He said to Romeo, 'I want you to stay by Swallow's side for a few days. Get to know your way around.'

Before Romeo had a chance to protest, Meribel appeared from under the wild tamarind. In her arms was a basket of cuttings, the fantastical colours of orchid petals.

'The humidity controller isn't working,' she said. 'Haven't you had a chance to look at it?'

The question was to Blanchard, but she was looking at Romeo, taking him in, before returning my gaze, and pulling a strand of hair from between her lips.

I knew why Romeo was here now, but who was he, I wondered, and what did he really want? I didn't have the answers to those questions at the time. I'm not sure I ever will. It's true that you meet people on the journey. They come and go. I guess you just don't realise until a long time after how they changed the direction of your life, or impacted it beyond recognition for that matter.

'Meribel,' Blanchard said, raising his voice, 'meet the new man.'

Later in the morning, I filled the flatbed of the truck with a number of clay pots which were beyond repair. They joined smashed glass panels, bags of refuse and an old bent-out-of-shape cast-iron gate.

The soil which bedded the assortment of trash was dank. Already it stank of growth and decay. Small discarded seedlings struggled in the rust-holes and crevices of the truck. They were the stuff of desperate survival.

Romeo helped me with the loading. He carried one thing after another. His demeanour was brusque, his movements measured. He threw one bag of compost into the truck like it was a corpse, returned to the debris and viewed it with something like disgust. Each one of his movements said, this is not what I am here to do.

At some stage during the season we'd build a burn-pile, throw a whole heap of stuff onto it that we didn't want around anymore, but there was a long time to go before then. Right now, Blanchard wanted the place tidied. 'Shipshape, and straightened up.' There was no point in hanging on to anything he might consider junk.

It would only entertain his unpredictability, and possible ire. And who knows how that would end up.

'Where are we taking this stuff?' Romeo asked.

'Harper's,' I said.

I knew an old Seminole who would be interested in the kind of matter we had – a curious old soul named Harper. He lived on the edge of the reservation, several hundred acres of land where the tribe had settled, and on which over the years a casino, hotel and museum had been built. We called it the rez.

Harper's shack was on the edge of the cypress swamp. It was made out of crushed beer cans, and the memorabilia of what had once been Seminole life. He built sculptures out of things people didn't want: bottles, mattresses, old air conditioners, radiators, pipe-work, anything he could salvage from the junk thrown to the side of the road, or left on the dusty pavements, or discarded across the wastelands of the rez. Blanchard had been to Harper's a few times and liked to call his yard-art cockamamy.

One small statue he'd made of odds and ends was of John Horse, a black Native American who had fought bravely during one of the Seminole Wars. I guess on some level Harper related to Horse. As a black Native American himself, Harper hadn't been fully integrated into either community. Harper was proud of the fact that he'd used his Marine-issued Ka-Bar knife to carve the statue. There was John Horse, arms akimbo, in the front yard inside a smashed TV. 'Some people call it outsider art,' Harper liked to chuckle. 'Outsidda what?'

Before I started the truck, I popped the hood. The engine was old. It had been repaired many times, but it was still running. I slid the dipstick through my fingers. There was sufficient oil, I reckoned, to get us to where we were going and back. That was good enough. I closed the hood.

'Why are we disposing of all this when we could be doing lab work,' Romeo wanted to know.

I said, 'I guess this stuff needs to go.'

'But there are more important things.'

'Maybe there are.'

Interesting that he brought up the lab, I thought. I knew Romeo was right. At least about the clean-up. But I also knew there was no use in debating the point. Lab work to follow, I thought to myself, once the ghost orchid has been located.

Romeo looked displeased, but it didn't stop him working. I noticed the cowboy boots were gone. He was strong, and he put his strength to use, heaving one bag after another, throwing them onto the cargo bed of the truck with a lack of care which bordered on the reckless. Still, I couldn't complain, he got the job done.

When we were taking a breather, I asked, 'What did you study in Belize?'

'Agricultural engineering,' he said.

'So you know plants?'

'I guess.'

'And you know how to grow the ghost?'

'Blanchard told you?'

'He told me some.'

He stood back and wiped the sweat from his brow. 'If you can get it, I can grow it.'

I smiled.

'I thought it would be here,' he said.

'That's what Blanchard said?'

'That's what he said.'

The sun rose higher into the sky, and the day became warmer. Over the years, my body had gotten used to its unforgiving power. Long gone was the heat rash, the burns and blisters – the insomniac nights of pain and discomfort. Now the sun met my skin like an old friend.

It protected me. I was so accustomed to it that whenever the temperature dropped even a little, I felt the cold, and I hated the cold more than anything.

Miguel approached. 'Pick me up something, amigo,' he said, looking to the ground before him, and holding out a closed fist like some kind of geriatric prize fighter. I knew what he was grasping.

'You know I can't do that,' I said.

'I don't want *that*.'

I knew he smoked weed. It made him lazy. But I didn't mind too much. It was the harder stuff, the meth, which was the problem. Any dealers who supplied him were wary. He'd gotten behind in his payments and had tried once or twice to sell product at the Garden. I'd managed to keep this from Blanchard, but I didn't want it happening again.

His hand reached out to me.

'Not that?' I said.

'I want tequila,' he said, his grip on the dollar bills loosening.

'Tequila?'

My hand went to his.

'Sí.'

'Tequila, I can do,' I said, pushing his hand away. I knew why he couldn't get it himself. I didn't need to look at the money in his hand to see that. He didn't have enough. He knew that, and I knew that. It had happened before. He was asking me to sub him, which I had no problem doing. Miguel had my back, and I had his.

He put his hand in his pocket, squinted into the sun and smiled, then glanced over to Romeo, who'd finished loading the truck.

'You here long?' Miguel said, by which he meant, 'Will you be here a long time?'

They could have spoken Spanish to one another, but they chose not to. Romeo answered with a shrug.

Miguel stuttered, 'You're here for the orchids, right?' He was grinning, looking to be helpful, and to make a new ally.

Romeo stopped kicking at the dirt but didn't look up. 'For the clean-up,' he said.

Miguel made a sucking sound.

'And yes,' Romeo conceded, 'for the orchids too.'

Romeo was being careful. He was right to be. Blanchard didn't want everyone to know what he was willing to do to save the Garden. But Miguel was sly, and he'd put together whatever morsels of information I'd let slip and had started to figure a few things out. Miguel nodded and the two men looked at one another again, sizing each other up.

'We need you, hombre,' he said.

He walked away with that languorous, slouching quality about him, kind of like a lame horse who'd escaped a bullet. 'Welcome,' he called out, 'to paradise.'

I guess that was his way of helping Romeo settle in. He'd not robbed him, which was something. He may even have felt like he was doing what he was told. Then Romeo and I got into the truck. Even with the devastation the hurricane had wreaked, the Garden remained, in my mind, a haven. I looked onto the black olive and the jacaranda's purple blossom as if they were the Garden's sentinels. And on mornings like this, despite the nursery's failing fortunes, it gave me what I believed was a special access into the pure beating heart of life.

The roads to the city were narrow, hard and unforgiving. We were still a distance from the looping maze of highways, passing one farm after another, and I was glad to be as far from them as possible. I preferred to be closer to the mangroves and everglades, to the land in its natural habitat. Sometimes it felt like I'd been travelling to get here my whole life, and sometimes I just felt trapped by the beauty, and the sun, and by something else I didn't even know the name to.

Romeo remained silent. I studied his angular face. Pensive, sallow and troubled, he looked as if he didn't know how to shake the shadow of a malaise. He was agitated, and his agitation only grew the closer we got to the city. The neon metropolis shimmered in the distance. It looked like a mirage of metal and glass, a landscape which the creeping, come-again vegetative life was on its way to reclaim, as though we were merely food for thought, for no thought.

He rolled down the window. Wind rushed into the truck. We drove on, past Redland, out by Homestead, but I knew the roads well enough to speed, so that the fields on either side of us became a blur of colour.

The rows of ploughed farmland appeared parched. Workers raised their heads and watched us pass. Then a field of pumpkins came into view, green and orange, followed by fields of blazing sunflowers. The air was still. In the distance, I could make out a stream of cars driving in and out of the casino.

'Business is good,' Romeo said, noting the traffic.

'I don't think it was ever anything but. Hurricane or no.'

I backed the truck up, and Harper emerged from his shack. The sun had scorched its surface, so that the paint was peeling like a scab. The yard was covered with all sorts. It was hard to tell what was art and what was junk. We got out and made our way to the front door. Harper came to us as we approached.

'Good morning sunshine,' he said. He held his hand out in greeting and smiled, 'Pahana.'

We shook, but Romeo held back.

'What's new in the world?'

'Nothing new,' I said.

Harper smiled and talked to himself. In his hand was a wad of till receipts.

'What you got there?' I asked.

'Testify. That's the name of the new piece. I'm making a statue of liberty out of these receipts, soaking them down into a paste.' He pointed to a bucket, and beside it a two-foot replica of the Statue of Liberty he was covering with the papers.

Next to the statue was some old hose he said he was making into another piece called Chutes and Ladders. 'Just need the ladders.'

I could see Romeo's brow crease with confusion when Harper bent to pick up an empty can from the ground.

'And what's that?' Romeo asked.

'That's an empty soda can,' Harper said.

I laughed, but Romeo's attention had been taken by the pair of dog tags that had slipped from the old man's shirt and dangled by his chest. Lord knows why he still wore them. I guess it's like that sometimes – we are accustomed to reminding ourselves of the worst of times.

Romeo and I unloaded the meagre cargo of off-shoots, detritus and mulch. All of it the old guy took gratefully, humming in his own way. I never asked him what he did with what we gave him. I knew he grew his own flowers – orchids, pentas, blue salvias. I also knew he grew some weed. I sometimes bought it for myself, sometimes for Lola, and Miguel. But Harper needed to be careful. The elders – Black Fox and others – did not permit him to do so.

I also knew he sold some of the pots and plants we gave him. He made use of everything. I asked him for nothing in return.

'He's here to take your place,' he said to me while shaking Romeo's hand.

Romeo took a step back.

'I don't know why I'd take your place,' Romeo said.

'Because I've been here too long, I guess,' I said, unloading more stuff.

Harper looked at what we brought him and smiled.

'That'll do. That'll do,' he sang. 'Chai now?'

He didn't need to wait for an answer. He served tea for anyone who came by. It was a special brew, made from an herb he grew – a mint-flavoured concoction which always left me drowsy.

To make it, he lit a small gas stove by the tree trunks we sat on. He took a blackened pot and filled it with tea leaves. Next, he handed us two blackened tin cans. In the distance, the sound of a souped-up car filled the silence. I took my tea, let it cool a little in my hands.

'Can't you grow anything up there anymore?' Harper said, letting the soil run from one of our pots through his fingers.

I drank the tea and felt the lethargy come over me.

'Not without your magic potions,' I said.

Harper picked up a few burnt lantanas and blue daze we'd brought. 'I can revive these,' he said. 'The others throw on the compost.'

I did as he asked and threw what he didn't want on the pile. We talked some more about this and that, and after a time, Harper spoke to me in his native language, a little of which he had taught me. He said, 'Your friend does not drink his tea, but he needs it.'

The wry grin, almost disguised on Harper's face, made me smile.

Romeo looked at me.

'What did he say?' he asked.

'Impatient young buck,' Harper said in his own language. 'Like the foals born in spring.'

He used his hands to mimic a foal's arched back and bucking legs.

The tea made me light-hearted. I began to laugh.

'What's so funny?' Romeo asked.

I didn't know how to answer him. I said, 'He has a name for you.'

'What?'

'A native name.'

'What is it?'

'Bucking foal.'

Romeo didn't even crack a smile. He stood, restless to go.

'He's here to help with the Garden.'

'You need help?'

'All we can get.'

'The hurricane was bad for all of us,' Harper said.

I looked behind him to his shack. How had it survived? It was nothing short of a miracle that it was still standing. The glass had been blown out, and the roof ripped off, but Harper had just got on with it and patched it up as best he could.

I reckoned our time was up. Harper had things to do, and so did we. I shook the old man's hand and said goodbye. Romeo and I walked to the truck.

'And you, what's your Native name?' Romeo said, climbing in.

'Harper,' I said, starting the engine, 'sometimes he calls me Pahana.'

'What does it mean?'

'It means lost white brother.'

Back on the highway, Romeo asked, 'How do you know him anyway?'

'Harper came by the Garden once, looking for an orchid.'

'How come?'

'He wanted something beautiful for his house.'

Romeo thought this was strange. 'He's practically blind,' he said.

'I guess.'

'What do you mean, you guess? He is or he isn't.'

'He sees things without seeing.'

'Oh yeah?'

'Like a witch doctor or something. He calls it blindsight. Of course, he could have gotten an orchid himself from the glades, but I guess he was curious to come by.'

I wanted to tell Romeo about one of the other sculptures Harper had made. A piece of aspen that was carved in the shape of a horse. It was of the first horse Harper had ever owned. He'd named it Tama, which means 'thunder'. But Romeo had lost interest. He hadn't noticed the sculpture on my bedside.

Instead he said, 'I didn't know a Native American could be in the army.'

'Marines.'

'What?'

'He was in the Marines,' I said.

Romeo shook his head — in denial or disbelief. 'Fighting for a foreign power, I don't know. He's a Native American first, no?'

I said, 'I guess he did what he thought was right. Or maybe he just needed the money.'

I liked Harper. I found myself coming to his defence. That was reasonable, I imagined. But not the swell of anger within me. Maybe it had something to do with the fact that Harper had fought in Vietnam. And that I too had be in the Marine Corps. Not that Harper ever really talked about it. Not much. He'd the thousand-yard stare. He'd told me once about one offensive, for example, where his whole battalion was wiped out near Khe Sanh. When he found his way back to base, the commanding field lieutenant said that he would have been better off dying. 'How are you going to explain how you survived when no one else did?' the lieutenant said to him.

'I told him I can't help it if I'm lucky.'

I'd laughed, but it was a sorry story. Harper *was* half-blind. Shrapnel had blurred his vision, and he couldn't go back to combat.

To Romeo, I said, 'He did what he had to do. Know what I mean?'

Romeo lit a cigarette. The smoke made me feel clammy. For a time, neither of us spoke. Then Romeo said, 'In Honduras, we have conscription.'

'You escaped?'

'I left.'

I waited for him to say something else on the matter, and for the anger I felt to die down. I didn't, in any case, tell him about my own time in the military. How I had joined the corps. Not as a citizen, but as an immigrant, which you could do at the time, no green card needed. I still ask myself how it had come to that. The truth is I don't have an answer. I could trace how I'd travelled to America from Ireland, drifted from one job to another, left a fairground in South Carolina and hitched to Florida. I knew how I'd been exhausted by the casual work, fired from one job, let go from another. I'd lived in a shed smaller than Harper's, been evicted and slept rough, but what it was that brought me to the recruitment office, I still don't know for sure.

Who knows why we do the things we do? I remember I had met another Marine at a bar, someone from back home. The guy had even gone to the same school as me. Is that why I trusted him? It shouldn't have been. He told me about the corps. He said it was worth checking out, and in a low moment, I suppose, that is what I did. I was in a haze of hangovers, but somehow they had taken me. I signed away my life for four unspeakable years, two of which were in Guatemala during the last years of its civil war.

They offered me another term, but I'd had enough. I took my honourable discharge in San Francisco, then walked. And I kept on walking until I found myself in one state after another. It's strange looking back, and I try not to, but I drifted, as if I were in a dream. And I hated that feeling, but that's how it was. Call it fate, call it whatever you want.

Then I was in Florida, by a bay, where at a dawn labour market, Blanchard found me. I know there are things I've forgotten, or can't remember. There are things I won't or can't say, but one thing I can tell you is how the nightmares of the war never left me. How at night, I would wake to find my hands balled into fists, sweat dripping from my brow.

'You left?'

'To Belize.'

'Yes, of course,' I said. 'How lucky for you.'

Krome Avenue came into view. Pretty soon we were outside a small mall by one of those strange off-road conveniences with a nail salon, Radio Shack, Chinese restaurant and bar.

Romeo asked, 'Why are we stopping?'

'I'm thirsty,' I said.

I turned the ignition off. The truck settled, then shuddered to a halt. I got out and walked towards the bar. Romeo followed. Two Seminole men were leaving as we approached. One of the men was smoking. I knew him; his name was Logan. I was wary. There were rumours about him being a troublemaker. He'd already been to the Everglades Correctional Institution for dealing drugs where, it was said, he had lost one of his eyes in a fight with another inmate. Miguel had had some truck with him, I knew that – dealings. The lost eye gave him a real sense of menace. He wore no prosthetic. Neither did he have an eyepatch. What you were left with was a dark hole in his head. He kind of wore it like a badge of honour, the way he zoned in on you and scowled. He always gave me the impression he was on edge, about to react, and unlike many others in his tribe, he did not wear his hair long, but had it shaved. But more shocking than that was the face of a wolf inked onto his chest, its head and snout snarling from beneath his unbuttoned shirt.

Both men's eyes were rheumy with drink. Romeo kept his distance, even when the two looked over to him. I spoke to them briefly.

'Who's your friend?' Logan asked.

'New help,' I said.

'You need it, I hear.'

'Sure enough.'

We talked about the weather, the hurricane and its aftermath. The men shrugged. I knew the casino had miraculously been left untouched. There were jokes made by the Seminoles that the rez looked like a hurricane had been through it before it had even made landfall. 'So, no diff now.'

But that wasn't true. The public-facing side of the rez, the casino and hotel, survived, but the Seminole's homes had been beset by a series of disasters. Once, when I'd visited in the aftermath of the hurricane, I saw an upturned school bus, and several toppled Ficus trees. The ceilings to a number of the standalone units had collapsed, their roofs caved in. Fences had been downed, and electrical wires were strewn about. The place looked like a warzone.

'Your boss wants to talk business?' Logan said.

'I guess.'

'Then let's talk business.'

'Sure,' I said. 'We'll be in touch.'

Logan and his friend got into their truck and drove off, dust rising in their wake.

In the bar, the neon was buzzing. It gave the place a lonely feel. Romeo and I could've been two ghosts who'd wandered in lost. There were TVs everywhere you cared to look, playing mostly sports – college football, basketball, greyhound racing. Colour and sound, wall to wall. The noise was almost pleasurable. It was such a change from the meditative rhythm of the Garden and its many silences.

The smell of food nearly made me weak. A charcoal barbeque smoked out back, and the smell of wood-chipped mesquite wafted towards us. I sat down, ordered a burger, and asked Romeo what he wanted.

'When you were talking to the natives, what did you mean by business?' he asked.

'We sometimes work with the rez on one thing or another.'

He considered what I'd said, brought his hand to his jaw.

'Procurement?'

'Sometimes.'

'I was brought here to work in the lab, right?'

'Yeah.'

'But no one has brought me to the lab.'

'It's not ready.'

Romeo shook his head; he read the menu, turned it over, read it again.

'Can't make up his mind,' a voice said.

A figure appeared from the storeroom smiling. It was Lola. I thought I'd recognised her voice, hadn't known she'd be here for sure, but something in the back of my mind must have hoped she would be. There were countless bars we could have stopped at, and there was precious little to distinguish them from one another. Soulless watering holes all. But this is where I brought us – where Lola sometimes worked. A bar called Deckards.

She stepped before me and laid her hands onto the bar top.

'I keep telling him it ends the same way,' I said.

'Hello, stranger.'

She reached out; briefly her hand touched mine. I noticed the nail polish. It was red and dark. It was unfinished. It was always unfinished.

She looked much the same. A different tint to her hair. Darker, blacker maybe. But that could've been the artificial light of the bar. Her face was as bright as ever, even with the make-up she wore. The sleeplessness in her eyes was there, sure – her insomnia ever-present. Her eyes, a dark and mesmerising green. Her smile, infectious.

She opened two bottles of beer, told us they were on the house.

'You're back?' I said.

It had been over three months. I'd heard little to nothing from her.

'Never left,' she said.

She was lying, and she knew I knew.

I said, 'I assumed you'd headed home.'

I drank my beer. The last time I'd seen her, we'd argued. We were on South Beach, taking in the sights, drinking. We'd no plan to the night, which is the way we liked it. At some stage, sitting at a beachfront bar, she'd called me controlling or something along those lines. I don't know why. It came out of the blue. Maybe I'd asked her where she'd been the night before. We'd argued some more. About what, I can't remember. She got talking to a group next to us, and later she went off with them. I went home alone. In the interim, I hadn't called her, and she hadn't called me.

I knew she often returned home to Chicago, where her parents lived. They were divorced. Her mother lived alone. Her father had remarried. She liked to check in with them, pick up money from her old man, hang out with her sisters, and take care of her mother, who had lost her mind. Sometimes, she'd be gone for months at a time.

'Chicago?' I said.

'My mother.' She lowered her eyes. 'I don't know how she raised us when she can't even take care of herself.'

'What now?'

'Diabetes complications.'

'Serious?

'Coma.'

'Sorry.'

A couple left the bar. The woman seemed to be holding the man up. She was telling him that everything was going to be okay. I felt the alcohol bring me down a notch. Out of the corner of my eye, I saw Romeo knock back his beer. Lola placed a small cup of peanuts before us.

'Who's your new friend?' she asked as if we'd been speaking regularly, as if we'd just picked up where we'd left off, which in many ways was how it was with us. Romeo reached for the nuts.

'Why don't you ask him? He won't bite,' I said.

Lola stood back and folded her arms and said to me, 'How do you know?'

Romeo took a quarter between his fingers and spun it on the bar top. He drank from his beer and looked at Lola, then at the photo of her which hung on the wall behind.

'Maybe I do,' he said, with such deadpan alacrity, I couldn't tell if he was joking or not.

'I can't imagine you're here for the ambience.'

Romeo didn't seem to understand.

'I'm here for the orchids,' he said.

'I thought the storm took 'em all.'

Lola was having fun with him, but he didn't see it.

'Yes,' he said. 'I'm here to help.'

'A regular Samaritan.'

Romeo looked to me as if to suggest, 'what do I say to that?'

'He's got skills,' I said to Lola. 'Blanchard hand picked him.'

'Like an exotic fruit.'

She wiped the glass in her hand, and Romeo looked away.

'He knows about breeding the ghost,' I said.

'The ghost?'

'Remember I told you about it — rare, beautiful, priceless.'

Lola put the glass down. 'Oh yeah?' she said.

'The Garden needs something to help get it back on its feet after the hurricane.'

'Right,' she said.

The expression on her face changed. A kind of glazed look came over her, and it seemed like she was seeing through me. I thought of Javier. He'd been an old friend of ours who'd gone missing during the hurricane. No one knew if he'd perished or if he'd taken off. We knew he had gambling debts, so it was always a possibility that he'd simply up and left. But we never found out. In some ways, there were plenty like Javier. People came and went all the time. Everyone was a transient. No one put down roots here. Besides, the roots had nowhere to go. Not even the mangrove seemed to have fixed roots in Florida. Still, Lola had liked Javier, and so had I. And now he was gone.

'We all need something to get us through,' Lola said. 'Anything, in fact. Hurricane or no.'

Romeo watched her carefully. He seemed to be intrigued by her, which was no surprise to me. I'd seen Lola put others under her spell before, men and women both. I could count myself in that category, I guess. Romeo was no different.

He raised his glass, 'Here's to anything,' he said, and downed his drink.

I called another round. My habit was to pay before I left, not drink by drink, but Romeo had his own way of doing things and threw dollar bills onto the bar top. He pointed at the money and raised his finger to Lola. He was tipping her, and he was letting her know it.

She poured herself a shot, and two for us. Tequila. The wrong time of the day for it. Still, we followed her lead and downed the shots. Then, a woman walked into the bar. She sat, placed her handbag before her, and ordered vodka neat. She took the blonde wig she was wearing from her head. She sipped her vodka, and her body shivered. She looked about her, then took a long tortoiseshell comb from her handbag. She picked the wig up and began to comb it.

Romeo said, 'You think it will make the difference?'

'What?' I said.

Romeo looked in the bar-mirror. He regarded his reflection.

'The ghost.'

'It doesn't matter what I think.'

'No?'

'It matters what Blanchard thinks. He's the one who hired you.'

The light was already fading. The day was on the wane.

We drank some more. Romeo ordered a burger. We ate. Then I went to the bathroom. When I got back Romeo was talking with Lola, making her laugh. As I took my seat, she began to tell him some story about Chicago.

'Can't take the winters,' she said. 'Coldest place you'll ever spend Christmas.'

'Snow?' Romeo asked, leaning towards her.

'More than you've ever seen in your life.'

He shrugged, then smiled. 'I've never seen snow in my life.'

'What?' she said. She stood back and appraised the man before her. 'Fuck off!'

Romeo put his hand on his heart. She shook her head and served us another drink.

'You'll have to come to Chicago sometime so.'

'Chicago?' he said. He smiled, pointed at me and winked.

I sat. Romeo took his quarters and went to the jukebox to play a few tunes. I told Lola about how once my dad had got mad at something. I don't know what. He was tired, our mother had passed away that year. To teach us a lesson, he put my brother Jamie and me outside. I said, 'Into the yard' and the words felt foreign on my tongue. It was winter, I told her. And it was snowing.

'Snow,' she said.

I told her how we'd thrown snowballs at one another, and how after we'd knocked on the door, our dad had only come much later to open it. He'd brought us in and lit a fire. We were all friends again. Jamie had fallen asleep, and I'd stayed there with him when the old man went out to see a man about a dog.

Lola leaned over the countertop and touched my cheek with her hand. 'I feel less alone,' she said. Then, in a quieter voice, 'You should call by.'

I nodded.

'You still remember where I live?' she laughed.

'I still remember.'

Then Romeo got back and we finished our drinks. I said something like, 'We need to get back.'

But Romeo wanted to play pool, so we stayed and played a few games. Then I looked for Lola to say goodbye. But she was nowhere to be seen. She must have been out back, or maybe she'd even gone home. She was like that. A young man with a septum piercing and two sleeves of bright and graphic tattoos had taken her place. He asked us did we want to go again. I said no.

Romeo swayed as we went out the door. 'Where'd she go?' he said. He had a fist full of dollars. 'I wanted to leave her another tip. I wanted to hear more about the snow!'

The next day, Blanchard asked to see me. Romeo and I were rolling out the plastic sheeting for the greenhouses when Miguel delivered the message.

He held his hands together as if in prayer. 'The boss wants you,' he said.

I stood, lit a cigarette.

'What's up?'

'He didn't say.'

Miguel offered me his flask, and I took it and drank.

'He's in the house,' he said, and pointed in its direction.

It wasn't unusual for Blanchard to want to see me, but to summon me to the house was strange. Every so often, if he sensed I was getting restless, he would ask me over for dinner. Meribel was a great cook – she did callaloo, jerk chicken and a goat stew which was delicious. But an invitation to eat came once in a blue moon.

'If it's anything *importante*, you'll tell me?'

'I've no secrets from you, Miguel.'

He smiled, 'If only that were true.'

'I'll be back,' I said to Romeo.

'Ask him about the lab, please,' he said.

I wiped the sweat from my brow.

'I need to get in there. That's why I'm here, no?'

'Sure,' I said.

I walked the short distance through the fields to the main house. It'd been painted a pale green before the hurricane and was built in the Spanish colonial style with large windows, wooden folding shutters, a deck and lawn. We'd done a good job cleaning it up after the hurricane, but it was impossible to hide that it been through such a force of nature.

As I approached, I heard a wind chime and the song of a meadowlark somewhere in the hedge of trimmed oleander. There were the rasping sounds of jazz on a stereo from inside the house, and the air was sweet with the smell of maple syrup.

I knocked on the front door, called out 'Hello', and let myself in. The hallway was tiled and cool. I could hear Meribel on the phone in the kitchen. It sounded like she was in a heated argument. I went in, and she turned and held up a finger.

'You don't seem to understand,' she said into the receiver.

Strands of her dark and curled hair covered her eyes. She brushed them aside and smiled. I'd often seen her brushing her hair on the veranda. It looked to me like she was trying somehow to straighten the Caribbean kinks in herself, but it never worked, and she'd re-emerge from this ritual like a woman who'd woken from a tropical dream.

'We've been waiting over four weeks,' she said.

Her voice surprised me in a way — something about the unpredictable cadence of her speech, the echo of Trinidad, and the smooth, lapidarian tones always seemed to take me unawares. Maybe because its pitch was at another octave to the guttural grunts of the men around her, maybe because of its gentle assertiveness; either way there was something alluring about it too.

'I would appreciate it if you considered this a matter of urgency. Thank you.'

She put down the phone.

'The bank,' she said somewhat despondently. 'They are being less than helpful.'

'He wants to see me,' I said.

'He's at his wits' end.'

'It's about the ghost?'

She nodded. 'What do you think?'

'I'm not paid to think.'

'Don't be coy, Swallow.'

'I think if it saves the Garden, it's worth trying to procure it.'

'It's a terrible idea,' she said, folding her arms.

'You think?'

'I know it is.'

Blanchard appeared in the doorway.

'There you are,' he said. 'Something to drink?'

'Sure,' I said.

'I wanted to talk to you about the state of play.'

'What's up?'

'We'll have to let some men go,' Blanchard said.

'But Romeo's just arrived?'

'Not him,' Blanchard said. 'Others. You choose. Let four go.'

'Just like that?'

'I'm afraid so.'

'I didn't think things had gotten to that …'

Blanchard gave Meribel another look, and she smiled and went to get the drinks.

'It's bad, Swallow. It's worse than she thinks.' He let out a world-weary sigh. 'We've put our lives into the Garden. I can't let it go without a fight.'

'I'll do what I can to help,' I said.

'You've always been good for the Garden, Swallow. We value your contribution, you know that?'

'Sure.'

'But we need the ghost orchid.'

'Easier said.'

'Right. And we don't have the budget to go through … the traditional channels.'

'Please tell me you're not thinking of the Fakahatchee?'

'It's one option.'

'It's dangerous, and it would mean breaking the law.'

'Not if the Seminoles guide us to it.'

'And why would they do that?'

'We'll pay them.'

I looked at him sceptically.

'Or come to some arrangement,' he said.

Meribel returned holding a tray with glasses. Blanchard took one and handed it to me. It was lemonade laced with vodka. Blanchard's afternoon pick-me-up.

'And when we have the ghost orchid, we'll be able to reinvest,' he said. His eyes were bloodshot, and I noticed a discernible tremor to his hands. 'We can create our own hybrid – the ghost moon – unique and priceless. I've made a proposal to the Seminole.'

Meribel threw me a worried look.

'Don't you think there are less drastic solutions to the problems facing us?' she said.

'I'm not so sure,' Blanchard said.

The ghost was one of the most valuable flowers in our business, and he was right, it could make the difference, but they were like gold dust. Rare and beautiful, buying one through traditional channels was possible, but Blanchard didn't have the means to do that, not now, not after the losses the Garden had incurred post-hurricane.

'We can rebuild,' he went on. 'Streamline. Produce more upmarket varietals. Create a members' area. Export, build, grow.'

A members' area? I thought, Are you serious? What about fixing the cistern? What about seeing to the sewage? What about repairing the barracks' roof? What about paying the workers, regularly and more? What about clean drinking water, for Christ sake?

His obsession had begun after the hurricane hit. But the ghost wasn't easy to come by. It grew on protected land, with special access granted only to the Seminole. 'That's the loophole,' Blanchard explained. 'We get the Seminoles to bring us there. They have a legal exemption to harvest any rare plant life. And we are buying access to that exemption.'

How serious Blanchard was with his intention to break the law I never really knew, not until that year. There were many times before the hurricane when he'd fantasised about the ghost, and now that the Garden was in real trouble, his fantasy took on a desperate intent.

Meribel watched us, and our eyes met again. I was waiting for her to interrupt Blanchard, but she let him talk. Sometimes I thought of her as another of Blanchard's creations, something he had cultivated over the years in the lab, like one of his orchids. He'd told me she came from good Caribbean stock, whatever that meant. He made the remark as if he'd saved her and then made something of her.

She was beautiful and watchful: a distant, but defiant object of desire to the men in the barracks. I heard them talk about her. Most were discrete enough to stop in my presence, but others watched her with a mixture of desperation and weary disdain.

How true any of what I thought of her was, I can't be sure. The Garden didn't have any other women in it.

Certainly, she was the target of a collective male gaze, and how much this distorted the real woman was anybody's guess. In other ways, she was a prisoner, a woman under house arrest. Other times, when I saw her on the veranda, glass in hand, wearing a light and flowing dress, she looked more like a ghost or a messenger passing back and forth from this world to the next. I'd often heard her and Blanchard argue, and I suspected Blanchard of cruelty towards her. I'd no evidence – tears are no evidence – just a hunch.

I noticed a piano in the corner of the room, its lid open, sheet music splayed. A vase with a mosaic sunflower image was placed at its centre. Above it, a framed sepia photograph of a couple in a rowboat on a lake with a mountain behind them. I was trying to figure out if the couple was Blanchard and Meribel, when he said, 'I'm talking with the Seminoles this week.'

'Black Fox?'

'The same.'

There wasn't anything for me to say to much of what Blanchard relayed. I stayed silent. I listened. I fulfilled a role. I'd become of late a confidante of sorts. It's true I'd considered my options. I'd thought of leaving, of striking out West, or into the Caribbean. It was no secret, I hadn't kept the possibility to myself.

For some, Florida was the place to be. It represented the freedom they'd sought after dangerous border crossings. For me, it had become another detour to somewhere else. Wherever I was going, Blanchard had persuaded me not to go there. In his eyes, it was simple. The Garden needed me. There was Lola too, and I'd become attached in my own way to Blanchard, and to Meribel, who I'd felt somehow more protective of in recent months, and more drawn to.

I suppose the reason I hadn't moved on with my life was about something else as well. It was about fear. I knew

I couldn't go back to the world I once knew, to the country of my childhood, much as I may have wanted to. There were too many painful memories there. And so, all that was left for me was to keep moving forward. But recently I'd been consumed by a lethargy which weighed down on me and kept me, not from packing my bags – I'd done that many times before – but from actually leaving the state's borders, though no physical impediment lay before me. I was stuck, and what was worse, Blanchard, I sensed, knew it. Each sunset, however magnificent, represented to me at that time, my future, setting someplace far off.

'Romeo wants access to the lab,' I said. 'He's been waiting.'

Blanchard picked up a newspaper and, without looking up, said, 'There's a few things I need to tidy up before we let him. Give me a few days.'

The front page in his hands was about a black man who'd been chained to a truck in a townland not far from where we were. He'd been dragged for miles before being decapitated, and the story had been all over the news. 'It would make you ashamed to be white,' I said.

Blanchard put down the pen in his hand. 'Not me.' He finished his drink and went to his office to take a call.

I placed my glass onto the table and turned to go. Before I did, Meribel, who had walked to the veranda, beckoned me. She had sat into the wicker armchair, the ice cubes in her glass tinkling. A fan was raised to her face, and she looked across the nursery grounds. Her gaze fixed itself onto Romeo, who was hammering a nail into the shade sheeting. The fan closed in her hand. Slowly, she brought the glass to her lips.

She shook her head. 'I can't take him when he's like this,' she said of Blanchard.

It was not the racial slur she was referring to. It was his mania, this obsessive drive.

'If anything was to go wrong with trying to get the ghost ...' her voice trailed off, and I stood struggling to find the words to reassure her. Before I left, she said, 'Swallow, you should come for dinner sometime soon.'

'I'd like that,' I said.

I excused myself and stepped outside. To the west, the sun had broken through clouds. Above me a buzzard was mewing, clear and stark in the azure sky.

That night I lay in the hammock on the deck. The stars were out. I was tracing the plough above me, mapping the night-time sky, finding my way to the North Star. I did this every time I got the chance. There was something reassuring about counting the plough's seven stars, and finding my way back to Polaris, as if it helped to orientate me, to give me direction.

I was wondering about the future, about how procuring the ghost could change the Garden's fortunes, and whether I wanted to be a part of that plan. Sure, the ghost could help the finances of the farm recover. There was no doubt about that, but what would my role be? What was in it for me? If there was an answer in the star's alignment, I couldn't decipher what it was. I was seeking answers, but all I had was starlight.

Romeo walked out of the barracks and onto the deck. There was laughter from inside. He smoked and shook his head.

'How can you stand it?' he said to me.

'What?'

'Living like this.'

Romeo looked at the torn bags of potting soil before us. Amongst them, a host of terracotta planters, chipped and smashed. He kicked at a bag. 'Sleeping in a room with those men.'

The truth was, I was used to this kind of communal living. The military will do that. It will get you used to all sorts of things. There was talk of getting my own place farther into the glades. I'm sure Blanchard could have helped me with the paperwork. I'd even asked him to, but he wanted me on site. He needed someone he could trust – for security. Initially, I'd said yes, and he'd paid me accordingly, but I was restless, and Romeo's comment rankled.

'Not ideal,' I said.

'No.'

Romeo sat on the steps.

'Blanchard wants me for security as much as anything else.'

'You're the muscle,' Romeo said, flexing his arm.

I smiled. 'Let's call it a temporary arrangement. The other supervisors all left.'

'He keeps you sweet.'

'I guess.'

'How?'

I shrugged, looked away.

'It's got to be more than money.'

I suppose it was, but it was also something to do with how Blanchard and Meribel made you feel like you were a part of something. That you counted and were kind of part of the family. Anyway, I didn't really want to talk about it, so I changed tack. 'What did you do before this?'

Romeo looked at me as if he didn't understand what I'd said.

'Before I came here?'

'No, before Belize.'

'I worked with my father back home. He was a farmer.'

'Was?'

'He's dead.'

'I'm sorry.'

'Killed,' he said. 'By the police.'

'What happened?'

'It was a raid. My mother was killed too.'

I felt I should be careful what I asked next.

'What kind of raid?'

'The police in Honduras, they're like the military.'

'We call them the Beast here.'

'They want a cut,' he said.

'A cut?'

'It doesn't matter what you're doing, they want a cut.'

'But a cut of what?' I asked.

He hesitated, and the darkness enveloped us. All around, the nocturnal creatures of the Garden stirred. I waited for Romeo's response, but he didn't tell me what the police wanted a cut of. He looked upwards at the throng of stars and lit a cigarette.

'People do what they need to.'

'I guess.'

After a time, he said, 'And we need the ghost.'

I sighed, 'Blanchard's working on it.'

He bowed his head, and I said, 'But it's not easy to breed.'

'No,' he agreed.

'I've never known anyone who could.'

He blew smoke into the darkness.

I asked him, 'How'd you know how to breed it anyway?'

'My father taught me,' he said.

'Oh yeah?'

'College helped, I guess, but my father showed me …' he paused to find the right word, then rubbed his finger and thumb together, and said, 'the personal touch.'

The night thickened. Inside the barracks the men finished their card-playing and drinking. They settled and fell to sleep. In the main house, the lights were extinguished.

'Tell me,' he said, 'how will we find the ghost?'

'He wants to use the Seminoles. It's on state land, but they can bring us to it.'

'Sell it to us?'

'Right.'

'And they're just going to do that?'

'I guess. If the price is right.'

He let out a laugh. 'If the price is right.'

We smoked and drank some more. Later, Romeo said goodnight. I stayed in the hammock and fell asleep. I dreamt of when I was a boy with a TV flickering in the corner of a room. *Day of the Triffids*, Jamie and I hiding behind the sofa, afraid to look. The old man laughing and the meteor from outer space, and the labs, and carnivorous plants. The curtain pulled back, a flash of light. Trees and shrubs uprooting themselves and moving towards us.

Then the sway of branches, and the grass exhaling. And out of nowhere, my mother stroking my cheek, saying goodbye, all of us shrouded in the leafy vegetal mass of a downy green-black presence. Ghost trees binding my wrists and ankles with their roots. Gasping for breath then. Outside – nothing but the stillness of a city street, and the rain falling in sheets. The sound – something like fire burning. Then waking the next morning, breathless from the dream, into the Garden.

I lifted myself from the hammock and sat on the deck and drank my coffee. It was strong and bitter and black and before me the lab, barracks and glasshouses, the whole warren of disconnected buildings looked to me like a strange lost village of sorts. It may have been the dream I'd had, but it seemed to me that the glades were on the brink of taking back the land, of reclaiming what it was we had taken from them. I heard a cock crow and the sprinklers come on. It was time to get ready for another day.

That night Blanchard left the Garden. I guess he was trying to find a buyer for the ghost before we took the risk of taking it. The men drifted across the fields and through the nursery. Their work was done for the day. Music streamed through the fields. Loud Latin rhythms. Salsa, and merengue. Some of the men even danced.

A fire was lit, I stood with the men about the flames, sat when my legs were tired, and listened to their drunken singing. The later it became the sadder the singing sounded. I looked about them and wondered which of them I would let go.

It might be Felix, the Cuban, who was strong as a bull. He'd stayed during the hurricane and had worked all week in its aftermath without sleep. Or Hugo, whose laughter punctuated the working hours with constant cheer. Or Ramon, who was skilled and dedicated. Not one of these men was disposable. Not one of them did not work hard. Each and every one would have shed sweat and blood for the work they did, as much out of desperation as out of the loyalty Blanchard inspired.

Many of us sat all night with the fire as it died slowly. The night gave way to dawn. When the sun rose, the men walked back to the barracks arm in arm, like courting couples with their heads bowed down, mourning the end of night.

After a short sleep, it was back to work. When you're busy, the day goes by quickly. That's what you want as a labourer. You want to be busy. A whole day can pass and your mind remains empty. But I had had to let four men go. I went to each of them and apologised. They took the news without rancour. By sunset, they were gone.

That night, with Blanchard still absent, a poker game was arranged. A table had been cleared of plants, and the remaining men sat around on stools. Miguel got drunk. He swayed from side to side, a cigarette dangling from his lips. With the cards in his hands, he looked like he was about to topple over at any second. I let it all be.

Romeo had his arm about another man. Music spilled out of a tiny boom box, loud and distorted.

'Meet my friend,' Romeo said.

The man he introduced me to was grinning broadly. Short and stout, there was a deep and ragged scar beneath his left eye. He stood shirtless before me and held out a hand. I took it and he shook my hand vigorously.

'Catfish,' he said.

'We're not taking any new men on,' I said. 'Friend or no.'

He smiled. 'Does this always happen when the boss is away?'

'Pretty much,' I said. 'When what they really need is rest.'

'Relax, cabrón, they're just having a good time.'

His bug-eyes and sweaty skin gave me the creeps.

'You plan on staying?'

'Sure,' he said, narrowing his eyes on me. 'Why not?' It was a challenge, the way he said it, and he knew it.

'For a night …?'

'I don't know,' he said.

'It's not a hotel.'

'No, amigo, it is not a hotel,' he laughed. 'I can see that. And we're a long way from Disneyland too.'

The men who were not gambling stood about and talked. I heard the back door to the house creak open and saw Meribel step outside. She leant against a post and cracked open what looked like a pomegranate in her hand, scooped out the seeds and placed the flesh into her mouth.

I remembered briefly a story my mother had told me, before she'd died, about the Greek goddess Persephone, who was made to eat six seeds of a pomegranate by Hades, the god of the underworld. This meant she had to stay with him for six months of the year as his prisoner. Her mother had mourned those months, and on earth nothing grew. I guess I got lost in that myth while looking into the fire. I imagined Meribel as Persephone and the Garden as an underworld.

A firecracker went off. I don't know if she saw me or not, but Meribel threw what was left of the fruit over the veranda's rails and went back inside.

Later, Catfish came up to me and told me he could help. I asked him how, and he said, 'With the ghost.'

'We don't need you to do anything,' I said, stepping towards him.

'No?'

'No, and Romeo shouldn't have said anything about the ghost.'

Catfish brought a finger to his lips, 'It's top secret, I know.'

I made another step toward the man and pushed my hand onto his chest. Romeo came to his side then and removed my hand. 'What's happening here?'

'Nada,' Catfish said.

Romeo led him to the fire and sat him down.

The embers spat and crackled. Some men waited for the cans of beans and franks they had thrown into the fire to pop.

'I can help,' Catfish said, rubbing his blood-shot eyes. He held out his hand and beckoned me to him.

Here we go, I thought. But no, he'd something else to say to me.

'You know why they call me Catfish?'

A man began to sing and the party stuttered into the early hours. I looked into the fire, felt the heat on my face, and said, 'No, no I don't.'

He stroked the coarse whiskers on his chin. His eyes bulged in his head. I may have imagined it, but it looked as if his cheeks were puffed and bloated. His voice was harsh and hoarse like a razorblade. 'Because,' he said, 'I'm a bottom-feeder.'

Later, when I'd gone to bed, I still could not shake his dark laughter from my mind.

After work the next night, I went to see Lola. It had been a while since I'd been to her place, and I felt nervous and unsure approaching her door. 'You should call by,' she'd said. The invitation was casual, but I knew by the way she'd said it that she meant it. I picked up a bottle of whiskey on the way, and when I got there, I walked past the pool, and up the stairs, and knocked on the door to her apartment. The paint was pink – dirty, faded and peeling. The eyehole blackened on the outside. It occurred to me that, in her own twisted logic, Lola may have done this herself.

She was home, her hair down, wearing a robe.

'Sailor boy,' she said, answering the door.

I held up the bottle, and she told me to come in. She went straight to the bedroom. I followed. Dollar bills were piled onto the bed.

'What did you do? Win the lotto?'

'I did not.'

'You robbed a bank?'

'No.'

'You started stripping.'

'Fuck you. I worked hard. That's what I did. That's what I do, asshole.'

I surveyed the cash. 'There must be three-hundred dollars there.'

'More. I counted it.'

'You don't say?'

She got giddy, sunk her arms into the cash and threw it into the air. Then she lay on the bed and beckoned me over. I lay down beside her. Face to face, I asked her where it came from, 'Double shift?'

'If I tell you, you gotta swear to keep it to yourself.'

I smiled and crossed my heart.

'One of the waitresses showed me. Someone buys two drinks; I ring up one, put the money for the second in my tip jar.'

'Simple.'

'Yes.'

'Not worried of getting caught?'

'The owner is an asshole.'

She gathered the money up into two piles and put a rubber band around each wad.

'When do we spend it?' I asked.

'This is for a rainy day.'

The sun was streaming through the window. I caught the smell of incense burning.

'Not many of them,' I said. 'Not here.'

She went to get two glasses, and we sat next to one another on the end of her bed like two awkward teenagers.

We drank the whiskey straight, made small talk, until she said, 'Are you going to kiss me already?'

I did, and we made love, and it was like she had never been away, like we had never been apart.

Later we went to the dog track, and I guess you could say she blew her savings, but she was happy. 'Fuck it,' she said on the way home. *'Easy go, easy go.'* She gave a huge tip

to the driver and said there was no point in coming home
with small change. Back at her apartment, we crashed hard.

When I woke, Lola was staring through the curtain.
It was not quite dawn. She was wearing my T-shirt. With
the first light catching her face, and without make-up, a
little pale, her hair dishevelled, tied in knots and hanging
loose down her back, her eyes barely open, she looked
beautiful to me. I was going to say something else, but she
shot to her feet.

'Holy fuck,' she said. 'Those fucking bastards.'

She turned and pulled on a pair of jeans.

'Come on,' she said.

We stumbled out the door.

'What's going on?'

'They've come for my car.'

'Who?'

'The car company. Mr Ford's fucking henchmen. The
repo man. How should I fucking know?'

We jumped in my truck. There was no traffic. 'Through
the lights,' Lola said. They were red. I drove through them
and onto the slick asphalt. The light was struggling to
break through. 'There,' she pointed to the car ahead, rain
spitting from its turning tyres. What were we going to do?
Follow it all the way back to the dealership? Cut the car
off? Steal it back?

I didn't ask about the missed payments. There must
have been many. But I did drive fast, following her every
direction. We drove for another ten minutes as the sun
emerged. The slick rain on the highway glinting in the
light.

'He's turning in,' she said.

'But what are we doing?'

'My diary is in the car. There are poems in my diary.
I don't want to lose them because of some fucking late
payments. Poems and entries about my life, about ours.'

I didn't know she was a poet. I didn't know she would risk our lives in pursuit of their retrieval. I didn't know that her memories of her day-to-day life – or our time together – meant this much to her, that they were precious to her. I didn't know much.

When her car pulled into the forecourt of a gas station, I pulled in behind. The repo man got out and went to pay. Lola jumped from her seat and ran to the car. She opened the back door, reached in and pulled out a large folder, and ran back. 'Go,' she cried, and I took off. Lola looked behind to see the man returning to the car oblivious to what had just happened.

'Fuck you, repo man,' she hollered. Her smile was wide. She held the diary in her hands, and said, 'Now you can buy me breakfast.'

This was a victory for Lola. The entire event lifted her spirits. Whatever she said came back to the fact that she had won, that she had got one over on the nameless man, the corporation, the bastards.

We stopped at a diner. Breakfast was pancakes and Bloody Marys.

'What's wrong with you?' she said when the Bloody Marys arrived. 'You've never cured yourself at breakfast? Drink up, momma's boy.'

She kissed me on the lips, poured tabasco into her drink, then took a stalk of celery in her hand and stirred.

We spent the rest of the day at the cinema. We went from one movie to another, in and out, regardless of the start or finish, leaving whenever she was bored. It was some way to spend a day. We came out into the dark, sleepy and a little in love.

There wasn't much left to the night but the hum of the city, a stray car zooming through the streets, streets lit up with fading antic energy. Down the strip, even the late-night fast food joints were closed or closing. We passed a car crash – a wreck – two smashed cars, totalled, an ambulance, survivors, a man and woman standing close to one another, shivering and in shock. There were three police cars, lighting up the dark night sky – the reds and blues creating a kaleidoscope of colour and chaos.

We tried not to dwell, to stop, or gaze at someone else's misfortune. That was the instinct, but it was hard not to. We kept walking, but we kept looking behind us too. About the scene were dotted these fake candles: luminous yellow lights. 'Mourning candles', Lola called them.

We reached the end of the road. In the distance, the public housing, subdivisions and gated communities faded against the night sky. Beyond the residential sprawl was a less inhabited landscape: the real, the true, the unexplored. Whatever you wanted to call it, it was out there, but the sidewalk ended, and with it our walk in that direction. And so, we returned the way we had come. 'It's something I hate to do,' Lola said. I knew what she meant. Going back the same way you came. It felt like defeat. 'But it's never the same, even if it appears to be,' I said. This, Lola didn't accept. Sometimes, there was no arguing with her. She dismissed what she didn't agree with, and sometimes not even with words. Her silence was as much an argument as anything.

But it was something else too. Her beauty, her magnetic attractiveness, her confidence, her unpredictability, her recklessness. I turned to look at her. Even in the darkness, I found it hard – she was that beautiful. I averted my gaze, and we walked back. I can't remember what we talked about, if we talked at all. When we came to the mourning candles again, they seemed to be shining brighter in the night, and so we paused, but only briefly, as if in reverence to the thought that things were passing from our lives.

The car had been taken away, so too the survivors. Quick work, too quick. The police cars were gone too. As was the ambulance. Nothing, in fact, was left but the yellow candles, and the sulphuric smoke they emitted dispersing upwards like some religious offering to the night. But there was nothing religious about it, and we passed without comment. There was, after all, nothing to say. The mess had been cleared, and whatever injuries had been sustained, whatever fatalities were to come, life went on.

Coffee steaming in the early morning. Acrid on the tongue. Waking the senses. First the sounds of birds and men shuffling. The smell of earth, and the greenness starting to take back, or the swamp beneath us trying to reclaim what belonged to it – without human interference, all elemental.

The rough touch of the bedsheet, of the cotton shirt, of the worn leather boot, of the roughened sun-sallow skin of my body, ageing. The eyes the last to open. The light – last to enter.

Today, a day of work. Life outside still throbbing through the veins of the eyelids. The sun and the pump of blood in some kind of tidal rhythm.

Fall was on its way. Or what I'd once called autumn. *Autumnal frosts enchant the pool and make the cart ruts beautiful.* A line from a schoolbook of poetry. Strange how these things come back to us, even though fall wasn't really a season at all down here. Still, there was a lot to be done. I marshalled the men, directed two of them to weed about the trunks of the fruit trees. We didn't want rodents. Then I took a mug of fresh coffee to Blanchard, who was in one of the greenhouses.

'The lab?' I said.

Blanchard took the coffee. 'It's not ready for him.'

'No?'

'We don't have what he needs.'

I knew he meant the ghost. 'He still needs to see the lab at least.'

Blanchard looked sceptical. I sensed his pride was hurt. Anything he'd tried to grow of late had failed. He needed Romeo, but it was a bitter pill.

'Romeo's restless in the fields,' I said. 'Besides, it's not what he's here for.'

Blanchard nodded.

'He can prepare for when we do have the ghost,' I said.

'All right, then. You take him.' He gestured to the stalls around him. 'I need to keep on at this.'

He'd pointed to the contents of the greenhouse, out of which we'd sold to the public and buyers. We'd rebuilt it and called it *the shop*. Blanchard and Meribel were keen to get it back up and running. It was one way of staying afloat – without flouting the law.

In the past, buyers had come from all over – locally, state-wide, from the West Coast and the East. They came from South America, they came from Europe and Asia. The well-to-do, the rich, the curious, the dilettantes, the collectors and obsessives. They came in a steady stream throughout the calendar year. They came, they saw, they bought. Purchased the rich and ornate dreams, the engineered hearts of worth. And they always wanted more. The next one, the better one, the one no one else had, the rarer the better, the less discovered, the soon to be. These were the businesspeople of beauty, the purveyors of good taste and rare breeds. In suits, with drivers and money. With cheques, transfers and cash. For Blanchard, cash was king.

There was also the public. They were made up of amateur collectors, or men who wanted to impress their lady friends. A diamond was not enough. If it was a mistress, the orchid would be purchased as something to dress their sea-view apartment. If a wife, the orchid mostly likely took the form of an apology, pre-emptive or otherwise. And women collected too. The sad and lonely wives of the rich, the widows, obsessives and manics, the seekers. What did they think owning an orchid did for them? For some it meant more than beauty. Maybe the orchid leant meaning to the vacuous, post-religious lives they lived, and replaced the dead end of therapy with something eternal. Sure, there were women collectors, but not many; and even though the orchid had both male and female reproductive structures, the world of its commerce was tawdry and male-dominated. And so, the buyers came, and they were welcomed and courted and sold to.

Sometimes Blanchard asked me to show the clients about, and when I did it felt like I glided through the greenery, the words coming to my mouth unbidden. But Meribel was better at it. And she'd filled more and more of her time in the last year flirting with buyers, fanciers and collectors, seducing them into their acquisitions. But now there was no one coming to buy. And that was something, because shopping was a religion in America. I shop, therefore I am. The lack of revenue made Blanchard desperate.

Miguel was moving tables about, and Blanchard was giving out to him.

'Not there, there.'

Miguel nodded to me, smiled wearily and moved the tables to where Blanchard directed. I tried to give him an encouraging look, but it was hard not to think of the set up as something of a sorry sight. There were so few plants left healthy enough to sell.

It wasn't until later in the evening that I managed to fetch Romeo from the greenhouse, where he was consulting with Meribel on temperature controls.

'I have the keys to the lab,' I said.

Romeo smiled. 'Finally.'

'We're in the middle of something,' Meribel protested.

'Come on,' I said. 'You know he's been dying to get into the lab.'

Meribel let out an exasperated sigh. 'I do, do I?'

Romeo waved a hand in apology and we walked across the field to the lab.

Not just anyone got to see the labs. For most of the workforce, they were off limits and out of bounds. The kind of area that if a worker even breathed an inquisitive query about, they were ignored, or even silenced. They were told not to worry about it, and in no uncertain terms. In terms which suggested quite forcibly: do not ask again. Do your job, and do not wonder.

Up until the hurricane hit, it had been where Blanchard had spent most of his time. Like a mad scientist of sorts, he concocted and produced the orchid hybrids for sale. Since the hurricane, however, he'd spent little to no time in the lab. He needed to restock rather than engineer.

I opened the lab door and turned on the light. Romeo looked around. He let out a deflated breath. I guessed it was not the state-of-the-art facility he'd hoped for, or been promised. Trolleys, rows of jars, latex gloves, oversize tweezers, razor blades, twist ties, pots, more pots, fertiliser, lamps, and more lamps, filled the space about us. It all looked a little worn and unloved.

'It's not what you expected?' I said.

'It will have to do.'

He picked up a beaker, some test tubes, a syringe, and shook his head. He was put out and unhappy, but he let his silence speak for him. The man had an expansive vocabulary when it came to body language – he was fluent in disdain, dismissal and disaffection. It was articulated with the angle of his hip, an outstretched arm, how he turned a palm skyward, or opened and closed his eyes.

'I'll make a list of what I need,' he said.

He looked through the drawers and presses about us, 'But will he be able to get it all?'

'He will,' I said.

As I watched him move about the lab, it occurred to me that Romeo had begun to become a part of the place. And in so short a time. It wasn't a matter of habituation, in any case. It was more like he'd bled into the scene, his presence like a dye dissolving in water.

When I looked at him, I imagined his face was the face of an ancient Mayan warrior. And his dark eyes were the eyes of his father and his father's father. And his words, an echo of what had once been called out by his forebears to one another, in battle, at work and in prayer, in love and hate. And even when he knelt to the sandy soil before him, it seemed to me, he was shadowed by a thousand souls who had perished without his knowing, guiding his movements with invisible guile and grace.

The nervous, angular energy of the man had softened. His presence was accepted. The others were no longer suspicious of him, he was no longer suspicious of them. But the change was something else entirely as well, as if he belonged here, the way I felt like I had once. In some ways, it felt like he was taking my place, just like Harper had said.

He smiled at me and looked relieved to be working on what he believed he'd been sent for. Even if this was a somewhat amateur-looking set up. There was no white coat, and instead of sterilised instruments, Romeo took a toothpick in his hands. He stood over one of the sinks, his fingers stained with soil, reached around the roots of one of the surviving orchids, and placed it within a small jar, picked up a syringe and injected the plant.

'Here,' he said, handing me the flower to replace on the draining board. '*Ophrys lupercali*. It's a wild hybrid, needs a male solitary bee to do the business.'

I hesitated, then took it from his hand.

'But so many leaves and stems have been broken during the hurricane,' he said.

'You think you can repair them?'

'Look,' he said, holding another orchid up to me, 'there is bruising along the leaf margin.'

'And?'

'That's where an infection can enter. We need to paint the wounded spots with fungicide.'

I found the spray for him. 'Looks like Blanchard was good at growing the orchids, but not so good at protecting them.'

'To be fair, it was a hurricane, but you're right – he's been more businessman than botanist these days.'

Romeo held a toothbrush in his hands then, and used it to transfer the pollen from one plant onto the stigma of another.

'We should go soon,' I said.

If we stayed any longer we'd only attract unwanted attention from the men in the barracks. And that kind of thing only bred envy.

'Okay.'

Romeo made what looked like a mental itinerary, then cleaned out the beakers while I reached beneath a sink and took out a bottle of tequila and two glasses. I rinsed the glasses and poured the tequila.

'It's good. But these,' he said, pointing with the empty beaker at the plants before him. 'They're not enough.'

'No?'

Romeo picked up the bottle of tequila and shook it. He looked closely on the worm at the bottom. 'We need the *orquídea fantasma*.'

'The ghost.'

'Yes.'

We drank some more while silver moonlight spilled into the cabin.

'You've never seen one?' he asked.

I shook my head, and his eyes lit up.

'It's something to behold. I saw one once with my father in Honduras. We were hunting for wild boar, and we came across it in a forest, low down, unusual, right? And fantastical, like a tiny fairy ballet dancer who has sprung into the air.'

I imagined the scene, asked him what they had done. He told me they had taken it and nurtured it at home. 'It was like falling in love for the first time,' he said.

He placed a hand on my shoulder, 'Why does this mean so much to you, amigo?'

I shrugged. 'I don't know.'

'You could have walked after the hurricane, wouldn't have had to deal with this … mess.'

'I thought about it.'

'But you didn't?'

'No.'

'So what kept you here? Why stay?'

'I guess I feel like I owe Blanchard and Meribel?'

'Owe them?'

'They took me in when I'd nowhere else to go.'

I could feel the tequila seep into my bloodstream and cloud my thoughts. 'I'm not sure there is anywhere else for me.'

'Sure there is.'

I told him that I'd been in the military, that I hadn't renewed my papers and that I'd been drifting nowhere, losing myself in the sprawling and anonymous erasure of American life.

'Isn't that the dream?' he laughed.

'I don't think so,' I said.

'You could go home.'

I shook my head.

Romeo stood and knocked back his drink. 'After this, I'll move, go somewhere else. You should too.'

I envied him his certainty. I had been like that once upon a time. Gradually, the thought came to me that if we got the ghost, I would in some way be released, and free to leave the Garden once and for all. That I'd have repaid my debt.

We locked up then.

Last thing at night, I liked to run the checks, make sure the temperature controls and lighting were all set. It was a routine that put my mind at ease and helped me sleep. Romeo came with.

'Why orchids anyway?' he said as we made our way from one greenhouse to another.

'I don't know. Sometimes, it feels like I found my way here in a dream.'

'For me, the orchid is like God, or sex. Or war.'

'War?'

'Yes,' he said, and I thought about the bombed-out village in Guatemala where – amongst a dozen dead bodies, some of them my comrades – I had seen a clutch of wild orchids growing.

We stopped. I was so tired, dead tired. The starlight burned above, and for a brief and hallucinatory moment, it felt like I was looking at those wild orchids once again.

The next night, Blanchard was back. He came straight to the barracks. Romeo was in the hammock resting. I was sitting on the steps, brooding and smoking. I could hear the TV from the barracks, but neither I nor Romeo took any notice of the streaming news, both of us lost in our private thoughts.

Blanchard looked harried when he appeared before us. 'You two,' he said. 'Let's go.'

He was breathing hard and bent over to catch his breath.

'Where to?' I asked.

'The casino.'

Miguel and Catfish were at the barbeque, the smoke wafting into their faces, looking interested and a little envious.

'The casino,' Romeo said. 'Why the casino?'

'We're not going there to gamble,' Blanchard responded. 'It's work.'

Blanchard turned and walked; serious matters looked to be on his mind. Romeo looked disappointed, but I wasn't. I was happy to leave the gloom that had descended onto the Garden.

'Come on,' I said, and we fell into step and followed Blanchard.

Catfish turned a piece of meat over on the barbeque and said something to Miguel I couldn't hear, and they both laughed.

'What's up?' Romeo asked.

'I don't know,' I said, but I had an idea. 'We'll see.'

At the house, Blanchard told us to take the truck. He would take the jeep.

'What's this about?' I asked.

'We're meeting with Black Fox.'

'About the ghost?'

He didn't answer, and I gave him a look. He said, 'You make your own way back. I've got somewhere else to be,' though I suspected he simply did not want us to drive with him.

Romeo clapped his hands together.

'I'll see you in the foyer,' Blanchard said, and we set off.

To be honest, I didn't much like the casino. Sure, there was something numbing and pleasurable about getting lost in its pinging maze of make-believe, but I'd been too many times before and lost. Many of those times were with Lola. 'I need the money,' she'd say. 'I'm short on rent.' When I offered to dig her out, she said no, that she'd never borrow money from a friend. 'Consider it a gift,' I'd say. Once or twice, she did take the money, shyly, and after a brief moment of effusive affection, she would revert to normal, relations restored, and act as if no transaction had taken place. But there were other times when her dizzy optimism to win swayed me. 'I can feel it,' she'd say. 'I'm sure of it. We're gonna win.' That or I just wanted to be near her. Because we never won, and leaving the casino after you'd lost six months of wages made you reckless and a little crazy.

'Black Fox is one of the Seminoles?' Romeo said on our way.

'A chief.'

We parked in a large lot that was half full. Ahead of us was the casino, a large anonymous building. It could have been a cattle-shed, but for the sad fizz of neon on its front.

'What circle of hell is this?' I said, and Romeo went, 'huh?'

We went in. Blanchard was there, waiting in the foyer.

'Follow me,' he said. He approached a reception desk and asked to see Black Fox. Pretty quick the Seminole appeared. He was wearing a suit and cowboy boots. He held out his hand to Blanchard and they shook. Blanchard introduced us.

'Pleased to make your acquaintance,' Black Fox said. 'I've seen you here before.'

'You'll have seen all the money I've lost then,' I said.

Black Fox shook his head and laughed. 'Not that much.'

He inspected his cigar. 'You've been here with a beautiful woman.'

I must have looked surprised. 'We have cameras everywhere in here,' he said pointing to a fixture like an eyeball in the ceiling. 'We see these things. We see everything.'

He described Lola. He said she had a lot of energy, and that she walked from table to table. 'She counts her chips again and again.'

I listened attentively. 'Sure,' I said.

Then he said he thought he'd seen her somewhere else as well.

'Oh yeah?'

'Dancing,' he said. He kind of smiled so that I could see his artificially brightened teeth. 'Yeah, dancing.' I squirmed at the thought, though I'd had my suspicions.

'Black Fox is the director of planning and development,' explained Blanchard.

He nodded his head then and said, 'Follow me.' We went to an office inside the casino. A man I recognised was sitting at a board table waiting for us.

'This is my nephew, Logan. My assistant.'

He seemed to squirm at this description. His shirt was unbuttoned near the top so that you could see the wolf tattoo clearly on his chest. He stood and raised his hand in acknowledgement of our presence nonetheless, the missing eye in his head as menacing as ever.

'So, I've seen your proposal,' Black Fox said formally. 'And I think we can help you.' He asked us to sit. Then Blanchard introduced me and Romeo.

'Romeo is the brains,' Black Fox said.

Blanchard smiled awkwardly, 'Something like that.'

Black Fox talked about the rare and beautiful plants of the Fakahatchee, about their worth and what they meant to the tribe. 'Priceless,' he said. He said that his people would never want to do anything to risk the preservation of such a diverse and valued natural habitat, or its precious botanical beauty.

'Of course not,' Blanchard nodded patiently.

'Rehousing any plants from the Fakahatchee is something we don't take lightly.'

'No.'

'But if you think the procurement of the ghost orchid could lead to ...' He picked up a piece of paper, Blanchard's proposal I guessed, '"environmental continuity", well, then I say, let's talk business.'

'Good,' Blanchard said.

'Our people know the Fakahatchee better than anyone, right?'

'Right,' Logan chimed in.

'But the ghost?' Black Fox said. 'It's probably the most difficult thing to locate.' He held up his hands.

There was more talk, but it all sounded like bullshit to me. It felt like we were taking two steps forward and one step back. And I wasn't the only one losing patience, it seemed.

'Who'll bring us?' Romeo said.

'Guide you?' Black Fox corrected him.

'Sure, guide us,' Romeo conceded.

Black Fox eased himself back into his chair. 'I guess Harper knows the swamp best. If he's not making some strange art piece, he's poking about the swamp.'

'Oh yeah?' Blanchard said.

'I'd say it's all PTSD, or something.'

Blanchard laughed.

'Logan, go pour us all a drink.'

The nephew looked like he'd been insulted. Reluctantly, he went to a cabinet and found a bottle of bourbon and the requisite glasses.

'Ice,' his uncle said. 'Don't forget the ice.'

Logan was steaming. It was obvious he didn't want to be the waiter. He puffed out his chest and made a show of his annoyance, then came and poured our drinks anyway, but not without spilling some along the way.

As he went to pour himself a drink, the largest, he said, 'The old guy's half blind.'

Blanchard laughed and looked on the one-eyed man suspiciously. 'Coming from you,' he seemed to say. What he did say was, 'But he knows his way around.'

The aircon droned above us, but it still managed to feel stuffy and claustrophobic. Romeo said, 'He'll need his second sight.' I think he was trying to be funny, but nobody laughed. Logan, who hadn't stopped moving with nervous energy, splayed his hands on the table.

'Let me go,' he said. 'I know my way.' He drank.

Black Fox considered his nephew's appeal. He sighed, a sigh so deep and wearisome that it suggested they had been through this more than once before. 'I don't know,' he said.

Logan poured himself another drink and drank it down. 'You know I can.'

Then he walked to where his uncle was leaning back in his chair and whispered something desperate and intense into his ear. I don't know – maybe he was threatening him; he was certainly pleading. Black Fox brushed himself off, and sat up straight, and returned with a smile so forced it almost said blackmail.

'Okay, then. Let's try that,' Black Fox said. He looked at Blanchard.

'You sure?' Blanchard said.

'Why not?'

'No reason. It's just I thought you might ...'

'I'm a busy man. You can hear out there, how busy I am.'

The sound of slots, muzak, and the endless chatter of the casino seeped through the walls. We all knew what this meant. It was a gamble, one which probably held a greater risk than the ones which took place within this casino. Here, the house, which was the rez, always won; out there in the other world, it was no more real than anything else, the risk was greater, and the laws of chance were not with us.

'Right,' Blanchard said.

'Right,' Black Fox echoed. He held his hand out, and Blanchard shook it nervously.

Black Fox stood then, 'We have a deal.'

Then the rest of us stood; it felt somehow that we had been at a poor imitation of a religious ceremony from my childhood, or a meeting with the headmaster. Before we left, Romeo reached for the bottle and poured himself another drink. He drank it quickly while Black Fox took a yellow chip out of his pocket and tossed it into the air.

I caught it, then turned the chip over in my palm. It was for a hundred dollars.

'I can't take this,' I said.

'Sure you can,' Black Fox said.

Black Fox motioned to Blanchard, 'Now about the terms of our agreement.'

Blanchard pointed to the door. We were to go. Logan seemed to scowl at us before we left. And Black Fox said, 'Be lucky.'

Once we were outside, Romeo took the chip from me. We got a few beers, and I said, 'Let's play.' We went to the blackjack table and I played one hand after another, then lost fifty bucks so quick I sat back and drank. I watched other men lose, and women; I watched them throw money away like it meant nothing, like it was not their monthly salary, their savings, or their home. I watched them throw it away like confetti at a wedding. I watched them until it became ritual, until the gesture started to mean something, until I began to understand that it was a ceremony whereby one rid oneself of something which was unclean.

Some could afford it, others most certainly could not. I watched one man make a killing. I watched him bet hundreds, then thousands. I was dumbfounded. And the booze, the booze was free, to a point. The way I looked at it – the house had your money, and the waitress had your tips. But man could you drink.

Romeo said he wanted to try the roulette wheel. He seemed to know what he was doing. I left him there and walked up and down. I watched old women at the one-armed bandits, intent and zoned out. It looked to me like they were trying to pay for their grief to be taken away or something. The transaction was a trap, even when the alarm went off and one of the un-consoled found the coins they had fed the machine returned to them, they simply took the same coins into their hands again and fed them right back into the depository of insatiable chance.

I walked about the place in circles, like a zombie. The tinny music of the slots started to drill into my brain, and I drank so much I didn't want to drink anymore. I was dizzy. Romeo appeared beside me. 'There you are,' he said.

'Win?' I asked him.

'No,' he said flatly.

We left without seeing Blanchard. On the drive back Romeo said, 'I'm hungry', so we drove through a fast food joint and ate in the truck.

'Why aren't we getting the ghost ourselves?' he asked.

'The Seminoles are exempt from laws protecting rare plants.'

'Okay?' he said.

'So we're not breaking any laws by them giving it to us.'

'Giving?'

'I guess Blanchard is buying it. If we took it, we'd go to jail.'

'But Blanchard's got no money.'

'He pays you and me.'

'But for how long, hombre? For how long?'

I told him I didn't know, and he said, 'I guess money is not the only way to pay a debt.'

'No,' I said. 'And for all we know he may have offered Black Fox collateral on the Garden.'

When we made it back, the lights in the main house were quenched. Romeo went to his bunk while I stayed outside on the hammock and smoked. I listened to the wind make its way through the palm trees. On nights like this, it felt like it was speaking to me, as though I was constantly on the verge of working out what its breezy grammar meant, yet it remained just out of reach.

Then I went to bed, and for one blessed night, sleep took me, and I did not dream.

On the day we were to search out the ghost, Blanchard was laid out in another funk. He couldn't seem to rouse himself.

'What's wrong with him?' I asked Meribel in the kitchen.

'He gets like this, you know that.'

'Worse since the hurricane?'

'He won't take his meds.'

'Should I talk to him?'

'He doesn't want to be disturbed.'

Meribel said his instructions were not to postpone, but to report back. Catfish came with, and Logan met us at dawn on the reservation. He was at the playground, where he sat on a swing drinking a beer.

'Oh man,' Romeo said to me as we approached.

Logan lifted his head and stood. He hadn't slept, he said; he was too excited. We got into the truck and drove fast, Logan giving directions the whole time. I rolled the windows down, and the wind ended all possibility of conversation. That was a relief.

The sun did its thing, and pretty soon, as we came closer to the glades, it was up and shining. Before an hour had ended, Logan said, 'Pull over.'

It was a hard shoulder. Nothing in sight behind or ahead of us, swamp all around.

'We can't park here,' I said.

'Sure we can,' he said.

I stopped. He got out, and we followed. He stretched his back and it cracked, then he lit a cigarette, and took his bearings.

'Where now?' I said.

He didn't answer, but walked down a dirt path, which eventually led to a jetty where an old airboat lay tied.

'I don't know,' Romeo said, pointing to the unprotected propeller. His nervousness made Logan laugh. He jumped on and started the boat. Water sprayed into the air and into our faces.

'Now or never,' he shouted.

We climbed on, and he sped the boat across the river of grass, water soaking us all. He laughed and we entered a section of glades with higher grasses. It was too loud to talk, and I didn't know where Logan was taking us, other than that it felt like a south-westerly direction. For a time, we seemed to hover, as if the boats's base wasn't actually touching the surface of the water. It was a weird and magical sensation, until he'd throw it into reverse, change direction, and we'd slam down into the water again. Then, out of nowhere he found a hammock. He stopped, directed us off the boat, then pulled it onto the bank with Romeo's help.

We walked. Logan had no navigational equipment. He went by his nose. Every so often he looked into the sky for an answer, but he didn't share his methods for tracking the whereabouts of the ghost.

'What's his system?' Romeo wanted to know.

'Beats me,' I said.

When I asked him, he got irritated. When I pressed, he was aggressive. 'We know this land. I know this land. This land is our land.'

Catfish said, 'I know a song about that.'

Logan carried his own stash of whiskey. It smelled so bad, I guessed it was some kind of moonshine. He offered it to each of us, but all declined.

'Maybe that's what made him blind,' Romeo said.

Logan wanted to know what he'd said.

Romeo looked away, but Logan wanted an answer. He stepped in front of him and brought his face to Romeo's.

'I asked you what you said?'

Romeo nearly gagged. 'Nada,' he said.

'Come on guys. Save if for later,' I said, trying to be the peacemaker.

Logan shook his head. 'You know we're the only tribe that remained undefeated by the US forces.'

Romeo said, 'I did not know that.'

'Show some respect.'

As he walked, he smoked, a pungent kind of weed; and it made him, on occasion, stutter and stop. At one stage, he wanted to sit and rest. We all stood around and waited for him to re-centre, or whatever it was he needed to do. I think he used the word 're-orientate'. There was the thrum of life from the glades, a hum of the primordial. Birds called out, chirping and singing. There were ticking sounds, and sudden trills, and drills. Whining, and splashes, and within it a kind of ominous silence and absence of human intervention. No radio jingles, no human shouts, no car horns, or machine sounds. Just the overwhelming murmur of a waterscape before man had arrived; it was like we were stepping back in time.

Logan pointed out a nest with gator eggs – which looked lunar, otherworldly. One of them had cracked and a head popped out. Catfish reached his hand towards it, when we heard a gator growl. We hustled, moved on, stopped to drink water, and hiked through the swamp, nervously. I think Logan was the only one who didn't feel the kind of fear the rest of us felt.

One hour passed, and then another. We found the poplar ash, the tree which the ghost was supposed to grow on, but it wasn't there on its base. Logan climbed the tree, but it wasn't growing high up on its trunk either. It took so long, Catfish wondered if he was ever coming down. Romeo called it a wild goose chase, and I guess he was right. He was also right about what was moving in the water about us, a moccasin snake. Catfish, fearless, waded into the water, caught it in his hands, and swung it about his body faster and faster until he landed its head against the poplar's trunk with a thunk.

Logan came down. We forged on, but after hours of traipsing through the murky water as light was fading, I called it.

'Time to retreat,' I said.

'Not yet,' was Logan's reply.

'I think so,' I said. Catfish and Romeo were already walking back to the airboat.

'You've got to trust me,' Logan said desperately.

'We have. We did. It's time.'

'A little longer,' he pleaded.

'And then what? Another hammock? Another poplar? It's late. We tried.'

I knew his pride had been hurt, but I also sensed that he'd had enough. His head dropped; he talked about how his forefathers had lived out here, in chickees, how they had survived hurricanes better than on the reservation, and how they'd hunted frogs, but wouldn't eat them. He was tearful, and it's not that I didn't feel his pain and hurt, and all the things he and his people had lost over the years. It was more that we were tired, and the ghost orchid was beyond our grasp. And I wanted to get back to the Garden.

In the distance, in what looked to be a sinkhole, I saw the wingtip of a plane.

'See that?' I said to Romeo.

'Couldn't be.'

I thought I remembered something about a plane crashing into the glades some years previously, a small two-seater. I couldn't recall if the pilot or passenger had survived. It had been a singer and his son, I think. Catfish wanted to check it out, but I said no.

On our way out of the swamp, we'd found some orchid saplings of another variety, but nothing else of note. We made our way back through the sedge and mangrove, mosquitoes swarming. Logan was quiet and sullen, but he had conceded, and we found our way back to the airboat. He flew us back to drier land, where dusk feathered the sawgrass with a hazy light.

We docked in a different spot to the one we had taken off from, and Logan explained he was dropping the boat off for someone else. Then we made our way from the swamp, out of the water and onto what gradually became a dirt path and dry land, a circuitous route back to the truck, and then onto a street of sorts, one that looked almost abandoned.

In his hand, Romeo clutched a clump of crabgrass. He was talking about how he was planning on using it to ferment a home-brew.

'We could call it barracks brew,' he said.

Catfish liked this idea a lot. 'Barracks brew,' he repeated.

'This is not the way we came,' Romeo said.

Underfoot was dirt. Heat was held in the buildings' bricks – an old bakery, a barber's, and a row of residences which were boarded up and seemed to lean into the street. The sun dropped at the end of the alley, as if we were in a tunnel. Weeds lined our way, a welcome outbreak of foxtail here and there. The hum of the highway far in the distance. Wind soughing the sagebrush ahead.

Then from one of the houses crept a lame dog with long black ears. Romeo fell out of step and went towards it. I heard something behind us, then turned to look. It was a pack of dogs, all mongrels, rabid and menacing. They'd picked up the scent of the lame mutt, and once the lead dog began to scramble, the pack followed. Catfish and Logan looked startled.

The dogs passed us in a wave of heat and hunger, and the lame dog at the end of alley looked up slowly, dazed and unsure. It didn't know if what was coming towards it was friend or foe. And it didn't have long to wait. The dogs dived in, growling, barking, biting.

Birds screeched, and the mob of dogs went at it, ripping and tearing at the lame dog's limbs and torso. The lame dog howled in pain, its fearful cries echoing into the alleyway and the swamp beyond. We heard a human voice. It was a girl calling out. I looked towards the dog again and saw the silhouette of the girl. She had a large stick in her hand and began to swing it wildly at the pack of dogs, shouting at them to get.

We ran towards her. Finally, she managed to disperse the dogs. She knelt down with the lame one, ravaged now, and whimpering. Its blood spent on the alley floor. She talked to it tenderly, and gathered it into her arms, the blood smearing her cotton dress.

Romeo asked if she was okay, but she didn't answer. She wiped her brow and left a tattoo of blood there too. Watching us nervously, she retreated into a doorway. I looked down the alley behind us. It was darker now, the dogs all gone.

'Come on,' Romeo said. The girl disappeared behind a door, and we walked away, found the truck and went to drop Logan back to the rez.

'We'll try again,' he said.

Nobody answered. We were tired and sore.

'We got unlucky, that's all,' he tried to reason with us.

'Sure,' I said.

'You hear me?' He wanted the others to chime in.

'Yeah,' they said.

'Alright.'

He got out of the truck and slammed the door.

When we got back to the Garden, Blanchard seemed to think that the failure had as much to do with his absence as with Logan's ignorance.

'The guy's a psycho,' Romeo said.

'Yeah, I know. I think the only reason Black Fox puts up with him is that the kid's his sister's.'

'Right.'

'Next time, I come with,' Blanchard said.

'But we need Harper to guide us,' I said.

'Sure,' Blanchard agreed. 'Set it up.'

'And Black Fox.'

'I'll talk with him.'

The moon darkened. I couldn't help but think of Logan's eye socket, like a black hole sucking the universe into it.

The heat had created a haze, a haze I lived in, like a cocoon of sorts. Even when I woke in the night and found it difficult to breathe, that condition became something of a comfort. There was a suffocating safeness to that viscous skin, the bubble of my being, like an alien in the spectacular fecundity of Floridian verdure.

When Romeo appeared, the balance was disrupted. The layer of skin about the air was set upon, as if chemically disturbed. Static charged. Clouds gathered. The skies seemed to fill with one thunderstorm after another. Then one night the driveway was filled with dozens and dozens of croaking toads.

I saw Romeo and Catfish smoking by the house. I joined them and together we watched the toads belch and trill under the stars.

'You ever seen anything like it?' Romeo said.

Catfish made his hand like a pistol and shot at the toads.

'You're still here?' I said.

'I'm moving on. You needn't worry.'

'Good to hear.'

'I had hoped to be able to help you,' Catfish said.

'But he can't stay,' Romeo said.

Catfish made shooting sounds out of the side of his mouth then.

'We need a day off,' I said, 'from all this madness.'

Romeo considered what I'd said. 'Tomorrow,' he said, 'let's go somewhere.'

'The beach,' I said.

'With thunderstorms in the sky?'

'Forecast says they'll be gone by then,' I said, and this seemed to satisfy Romeo.

Next day was Sunday; we left Catfish behind and drove oceanward with the smell of salt and diesel in the air. He'd some business to take care of downtown. Fine, I thought. I didn't want him getting used to being around anyway. The Garden couldn't carry him, and I figured we were better off without him.

At the beach, Romeo and I bought towels and swimming trunks in a market and settled onto the sand. It was busy, but not packed. I went straight into the sea, and lay on my back in the water, staring up into the eternal blueness of the sky.

After a time, I swam some more then found Romeo in my line of vision and waved. At first, he tried to ignore me, but eventually he came to the water's edge.

'What are you waiting for?' I called.

He waded in and said something about sharks.

'Come on in. There's no sharks.'

Farther and farther he waded, slowly getting used to the water, enjoying its warm transparency, lowering himself to his chest. Then he dunked his head under and came up shaking the water from his hair and smiling.

I swam a little more, the smell of baked seaweed in the air. The tide was choppy and getting stronger. Then I saw a lifeguard changing the flag from yellow to red. I turned back to where I'd swam from. Romeo was standing in the water. He was up to his neck now, and I waved, but he didn't see me. I was going to shout out something about the flag change when I saw him dive back into the water. I waited for him to re-emerge so that I could shout out again, but he didn't. Not at first.

What happened was this: he kind of sprung up out of the water a few metres from where he'd dove, then I saw him being dragged through the water. He was flailing some, not even waving. I saw him take huge gulps of air before being pulled back down. It was weird.

I waved to the lifeguards, but they'd already seen him. Lightning fast, they sped out with their lifebuoys on a jet ski. One of the lifeguards dived in and found Romeo. He was barely conscious. They tied a lifebuoy about him, pulled him out of the water, brought him back to shore, and laid him out on the sand. A small crowd had gathered. Romeo threw up a bunch of water, and looked a little dazed, but when he saw me, he smiled.

He ran his fingers through his hair and looked at the grains of sand on his fingertips with bemusement. His brow creased, and I held my hand out to pull him up. He took it.

'What happened?' he said.

'Rip tide.'

He refused to go to hospital, so I said I'd take him home, and we wrapped him in his towel and put him back in the truck.

On the way, he said, 'Let's not do that again.'

'You should have told me you can't swim,' I said.

'Cabrón,' he said. 'I wasn't planning to.'

Back at the Garden, the temperatures dropped, and within days we were wintering, getting ready for the cold, its indiscretion, its disregard, nailing sheets of plastic onto the wooden, make-shift hoardings.

'There's a chill in the air,' Blanchard said, marshalling our efforts.

Each season, when I bent to the trellis and sheeting with nails, knife and axe, I wondered what it was we were doing? Or why was it that what we were doing was called *wintering*? I suppose it was self-evident. Wintering in sunshine, the past still growing toward the light.

I placed my hands by the firebush and felt the red flower's cold heat. Wintering: that the time of year had come around so quickly was something of a surprise. But what of it? In the Garden there was the cycle of birth, growth, decay and rebirth. I saw it every year, but this year was different. After the hurricane, nothing was growing again the way it was supposed to; every plant needed extra care and special assistance.

I planted seeds for beets, carrots, radishs and cabbage, then covered them with shade-cloth – a small crop to feed ourselves. The green structures about us looked to be more vulnerable, and starker against the earlier sunsets, and the sky's darkening vermilions.

The seasons revolved, slowly, and anyway there was only really two down here. Strange to have come from a quatrain of difference to a binary of wet and dry. Still, they seemed reassuringly to be a variation on a theme. Of degrees of heat and humidity. Of thoughtless labour and forbearance. My blood had absorbed the climate, and my heart beat the temperature about my own system, regulating it to a fetid pitch of sweat, and toil, and somewhere within that was the source of my own meek pleasure, and my safety.

Otherwise, we tried to carry out our duties in the same fashion, dutiful and obliged. Bar the seasonal shift, the axis' tilt, all appeared as it was, but it wasn't, and we weren't. Something had happened, and something had changed. Maybe it had to do with Romeo. With his arrival had come a sense of expectation and of desperation. We needed the ghost.

And it felt like Blanchard's obsession had become mine. I walked in and out of the greenhouses, through the shade-houses, and into the fields. Sometimes I wondered whose dream I was in.

That first night of wintering, I drove to Lola's. When I got there, I found a car idling at the gate to the apartment complex. The gate was stuck. A man was pulling it open with a mix of fury and despair. A woman in the passenger seat tried to reason with him. He shouted at her, and she sat back into the car, pulling on the ends of her long black hair. I heard her speak the Lord's name. When the man had finally prised open the gate, I followed them inside and parked the truck.

I rang the bell and knocked again. There was no answer. I leant and listened. I imagined she was in there with someone else, that I was trespassing. I was convinced I'd made a mistake, that I'd crossed a line. I turned quickly to go.

From the stairwell rose the smell of stale weed. More pink paint flaked from the walls. The apartment complex was grimy and unkempt. I was filled with a sudden pang of disgust. I felt queasy and cold. For a moment, leaning over the railing, looking down the five floors to the parking lot below, I thought I was going to be sick. A sweat broke out on my brow. The back of my neck was damp. The thought of bodies floating or flying through the air and falling onto the pavement below beset me. Bones smashed. Blood. It felt less like a dream, and more like someone else's memory of what might have been. Then, just as I was about to leave, Lola opened the door.

'Hey,' she said.

I followed her inside. In the corner of her room was a suitcase, and in the suitcase was a small mountain of shoes, toppling over one another – sneakers, moccasins, flip-flops.

'Having a sale?' I said.

'Funny,' she replied.

We drank. We smoked. The window unit stuttered and stopped. I felt dizzy with desire.

'Fucking thing,' Lola said, throwing a shoe at it.

For a time, we just lay on the bed.

'What are we doing?' she said.

The fan above us whirred in the semi-darkness. I didn't answer. The question was too much.

'What news from Eden?' she asked.

I told her about the swamp, and Logan. I told her we'd been looking for the ghost.

'You guys are crazy,' she said.

'Then Romeo and I escaped to the beach.'

'Why didn't you call me?'

'You would have come?'

'Yeah, I would've come.'

'Romeo nearly drowned.'

She turned onto her side and touched my face.

'Jesus.'

She seemed upset.

'What?' I said.

'I'd a sister who drowned.'

'I never knew.'

'Amy, she was my baby sister. One summer's day, my father brought her to a lake near where we lived. She liked to swim. He sat on the shore and dozed. She drowned.'

She spoke matter-of-factly.

'That's one thing we have in common,' I said.

I told her about Jamie then, how after my mother had died, something gave way in the old man, how he slept much of the day, how he didn't cook or clean. And that after days, or was it weeks, I remembered his sister had come to feed us. She'd scolded him, told him we were famished. I remembered the fights, and the bitter cold, the ice covering the fields and roads about us in a silver light. So, it must have been winter when mum died.

I could see my breath as we climbed into my father's car. He'd turned the key one time after another until the engine took, then blew onto his hands, while my brother whimpered. I remembered telling Jamie to stop his crying. I wished I hadn't. I wished I could have taken those words back. Of course, Jamie hadn't been told what my father was planning, but he must have known, somewhere in the back of his mind, but he said nothing, and my father had driven on without speaking, and in that silence the roads had appeared empty and desolate.

I was ten, Jamie nine. Irish twins is what our mother liked to call us. For a long time, I never understood that. Reaching out to us from her hospital bed, repeating what we were to her. When we arrived at my aunt's house, my father had told us to wait in the car. I remembered looking out the window at the fumes from the exhaust tunnelling upward into the stark morning air. Then the old man had rung the doorbell and when no one had answered he'd knocked on the door. After a time, his sister had appeared, pulling a robe about her. They'd argued, and my father's head had gone into his hands. I think he may have wept. He'd pulled an arm across his face, and his sister had reached out to him, then looked to us shivering in the car. My brother had stopped his shaking. He was playing with an old teddy bear mum had given him before she'd passed. He was talking to it, and I felt this deep brotherly love for him. Then, as my father had walked towards the car, this love was replaced by a queer disorientation, as if I were on a swing and someone had pushed me far too high. My father's moment of weakness, his tears on the doorstep of his sister's house, was gone. He'd opened the door on my brother's side and held out his hand. Jamie had said something, but I can't remember what. He was still in his pyjamas. They had a blue paisley cotton print. I'd seen him shiver and look back to me. My father guided him towards the door, then hugged him desperately on the doorstep. When he got back to the car, he said nothing, but sat for a short time while I looked out the window. 'Where is Jamie going?' I said. Then suddenly my father grabbed a bag from the front seat and ran to the door before it was closed. His sister turned and took the bag, and there was barely the blur of Jamie's blue pyjamas and brown hair left in my field of vision, barely the chance to say sorry for asking him to stop his whimpering, barely the chance to say goodbye.

I said to Lola, 'It was the last time I saw my brother.'

She sat back, shook her head, and drank.

'Fuck,' she said, then kissed me, 'what happened?'

I told her that, a few years later, as a teenager, he had taken his own life. For a long time, neither of us said anything. From the way we lay against one another, I could hear her heart beat. Her hand rested on my chest as if the contact was needed to keep her alive. That's how those moments felt.

Then, she spoke in a whisper, 'Once when I was kid my father took his gun and put it in my mouth.'

She sat up and started to undress.

'He cocked the hammer.'

'Lola?'

Her clothes fell to the floor.

'You don't have to,' I said.

She took the candle from the bedside table and lit it. She let the flame take and waited for the wax to gather. She let it drip onto the back of her hand, then tipped the candle towards her body.

'Do that,' she said, turning onto her back.

I took the candle and spilled the wax onto her skin, and it reddened, and her body quivered beneath me.

The next evening, back at the Garden, while I was spraying the bromeliads, Meribel came to me.

'Are you free for a food drop?'

'Now?' I said.

'Car's loaded.'

I put the sprayer down and said, 'Sure.'

As we walked to the jeep, Meribel twirled the keys around her finger.

'Blanchard know?' I asked.

She gave me a look. 'He thinks that by giving away leftovers to the homeless we compromise the integrity of the food.'

'What does that even mean?'

'It means he doesn't like it.'

We got into the car and drove downtown. It was something Meribel liked to do. I guess it meant she wasn't wasting anything, a charitable action on her part, and in another way, it demonstrated her independence from Blanchard. A small act of rebellion, you could call it. I'd been a few times with her before, not many, but it was a companionable time. She made me feel at ease, and a little more besides. There was none of the madness of Lola about her, none of the reckless, unpredictable danger which I felt I was somehow outgrowing. This felt different, like her heartbeat was in sync with mine, and the rhythm of our blood knew the other.

On the back seat was a basket with foil-wrapped tortillas. Meribel must have heated them up. They smelt warm and appetising.

'Everything OK in the barracks?'

'Sure,' I said.

'I heard about the beach.'

'He didn't tell me he couldn't swim.'

'And the lab?'

'He's happy enough.'

Pretty soon we made it to the underpass, where the homeless heaved and moved and eked out their nocturnal existence with something like dread and awe. Two men approached, one a short man in an oversized coat, the other a larger man with a white sweatband circling his head.

'You recognise them?'

Meribel nodded and got out. 'Grab the food.'

They smiled and talked. Meribel was easy with them. I got out then and took the basket with me. I handed out tortillas until one of the men took the basket from me and smiled. He handed them out to the others who were lining up until they were all gone.

'Thank you,' he said. 'What a bounty.'

Then Meribel talked some more with the men. She opened her arms, and the big guy fell into them.

'Don't be a stranger,' he said and laughed.

'I'll do my best,' she said.

And that was it. We said goodbye.

'You come back,' the man called out.

Back in the car, Meribel said, 'Swallow.'

I looked at her.

'Can you promise me something?'

'Anything.'

'I'm serious. Can you please not indulge him?'

'I can't make Blanchard do anything,' I said. 'He's his own man.'

'He trusts you.'

I sighed.

'What do you want me to do?'

'I want you to reason with him,' she said.

'Isn't that your job?'

She smiled painfully. 'He doesn't listen to me. Not anymore.'

I held up my hands.

'The ghost,' she said. 'Nothing good will come of it.'

'You don't know that.'

She stopped the car on the hard shoulder and put her head against the steering wheel. When she lifted it, her eyes seemed to be tearing up.

'Look, we had something good at the Garden. We put everything into it, but I don't know if it has a future. Everyone's suffering. You just saw it with your own eyes. Some of those people weren't homeless six months ago.'

'And if we don't do something drastic that could be us!'

'That's not what I mean.'

'I think Blanchard will do just about anything to keep it going.'

'Maybe it's time for us all to reassess.'

She looked into the rear-view mirror and drove back onto the road.

'You know I'd do anything for you,' I said.

She took a deep breath in. I hadn't planned on saying what I'd said, but I had, and something was out there now. She reached over and touched my hand.

'I know you'd do anything for him too.'

We both kind of laughed at that, awkwardly. Then she said, 'Take me for a drink.'

'Where?'

'Where you and Romeo go?'

I told her to drive to Tobacco Road, but with a touch of doubt in my mind. I'd kept these worlds separate over the last number of years. I'd liked the idea that there was the Garden, and then there was life outside the Garden – Lola, and the city, and whatever else.

My trip with Romeo to the beach had blurred the boundary between those worlds, and now I was taking Meribel out. It felt somehow dangerous to do so, as if one world didn't belong in the other. It felt as if I would lose whatever control I had of what would happen in each of those worlds if they somehow seeped into one another, but something in me capitulated.

The place was busy, the music loud. I walked to the bar and Lola came over and said hello.

'What can I get you?'

I ordered a beer. Meribel wanted a white wine, which made Lola smile.

'You're busy …' I said.

Lola said, 'Jesus wept,' and looked over to a group of men by the pool table. They were a ragtag mix of whites, Latinos and Natives, and they were drinking hard and laughing loud. Logan was with them, but he was standing apart, staring at us, expressionless and intent.

'There's a horse race or something at the rez,' Lola said, serving us our drinks.

'Oh yeah?'

'And a powwow.'

The energy from the group was unpredictable, their talk and laughter competing with the music on the jukebox.

'You guys work together?' Lola said.

I introduced Meribel.

'Blanchard's wife?'

'You know him?' Meribel said.

'Of him.'

The two women sized each other up.

'You two friends?' Meribel asked coyly.

Lola took her cloth and wiped the counter. 'We're acquainted,' she said.

I got the sense they were trying to figure out where we stood with one another. Still, I could tell they liked each other.

Lola went to serve another customer.

'She seems nice,' Meribel said, smiling as she brought the glass to her lips.

'I don't know if nice is the word,' I said, when I saw out of the corner of my eye Logan approaching.

'We'll go again,' he said, 'to the swamp.'

His eye was bloodshot, his voice hoarse. It was obvious he was pretty drunk. He was sore at his failure to guide us through the glades on our first mission.

'I don't know,' I said.

'Sure we will. I know where it is. It's not a problem.'

I looked away and Logan stepped closer, so that I could smell his foul breath on my face. Then he whispered so that Meribel couldn't hear him.

'Look,' he said. 'If you can make it worth my while, I can bring you to it and a whole lot else besides.'

I sat back. 'The financial arrangement is between Blanchard and Black Fox.'

'Black Fox,' he laughed. 'You mean Dunbar. George Dunbar, my uncle.'

'Sure, whatever his name is.'

He leant down and took a hold of my shirt collar. 'Look,' he said again. 'I can make this happen. Just pay me what you owe me.'

I pushed him away. 'I don't owe you anything.'

The man laughed, but his expression changed, so that his eye was dark and threatening. He was looking right at me, and I felt pinned to the wall by his stare. Sure he wanted money, but I guess his pride was hurt too, at not being able to find the ghost. And something about his gaze suggested to me that he was aware on some level that he had failed his forebears and become separated from a knowledge of the land his people once had. His laughter subsided.

'Who's this?' Logan said, turning to Meribel.

Before she could answer, he was pulled away by one of his friends.

'I know who that is,' Logan said, turning to the pool table. 'Blanchard wouldn't like it.'

I drank my beer, Meribel stared me down, and Lola came to our table with more drinks. 'A real charmer,' she said.

'Who was that?' Meribel asked.

'Trust me,' I said, 'you don't even want to know.'

The next day, I was outside the barracks smoking when I heard a commotion from inside. Romeo and Catfish were fighting.

I went in. 'What's going on?'

'He got himself recruited,' Romeo said. 'This man is going to be a US military man.'

'What?'

Catfish struggled free of Romeo.

'It's a job,' Catfish said.

Romeo mouthed something that sounded like 'idiot'. I looked at Catfish. He was grinning inanely, gold glittering inside his mouth.

'Sergeant says he can't go anywhere today,' Romeo said. 'They may come get him.'

'When?' I asked.

'At any time. Sergeant is worried he'll go drinking.'

Catfish giggled. There was something unnerving about seeing a grizzly bear like that giggling, the weight about his haunches and midriff jiggling to his girlish hilarity.

'He looks like he's already had a taste,' I said.

I left them to it, and things quietened down, but later that night the two men were fighting again. I guess Romeo disagreed with his friend's decision. The men called out for them to stop, to be quiet, to let them sleep. I joined in, and hollered, 'Shut the hell up.' By then Catfish had finished a bottle of tequila, and Romeo was trying to restrain him.

'Fool,' he called out. 'Back to your cot.'

They wrestled one another until Romeo freed himself. He found a vacuum cleaner we sometimes used to clean the place and threw it at Catfish. A wound above his left eye opened. Blood seeped out. We patched him up as best we could, fed him more tequila and put him to sleep. Then Romeo and me had a drink, and he sang some sad lullaby in Spanish.

'Let's hope the sergeant doesn't come to pick up this prize fighter tonight,' he said before we climbed into our bunks.

In the morning, Catfish looked penitent and battered. Romeo retrieved the mirror from the bathroom to show him his handiwork.

'What the fuck am I going to do?' he said.

'It's no beauty pageant, is it?'

Romeo apologised. Then the phone in the barracks rang; it was for Catfish.

He took the call, listened, and put down the receiver. 'They want me to come down to sign papers,' he said.

Romeo stood up straight and saluted.

When he came back later that afternoon, Catfish was sheepish.

'What did they say?' Romeo asked.

Catfish lay back onto his bed, 'They said I should stay out of barroom brawls.'

'You told them it was no barroom, I hope.'

'When I said it was a vacuum cleaner, they didn't believe me.'

We laughed.

'I needed stitches, man,' he whined in Spanish, before reverting to English. 'A whole lotta stitches.' He ran his finger over his swollen eye and the crooked line of black coarse thread.

'When are they coming for you?' Romeo asked.

'Tonight.'

He sat about for the rest of the day nursing his wounds, chain-smoking and drinking. He scowled at any man who looked at him.

'Going to ship you overseas?' Romeo asked.

Catfish shrugged. 'Bootcamp first.'

Romeo clapped me on the back.

'Ask Swallow,' he said to Catfish. 'He's done it all.'

Catfish turned to me. His eye darkened, 'What's it like, hombre?'

'It's not so bad,' I lied.

Romeo started to laugh. He spoke in Spanish and said, 'If you don't mind getting up at 4 a.m. every goddamn day and getting your ass kicked.'

'Mighty kind of you,' I said, 'to add the detail.'

Romeo blew smoke rings in the air, and then in a mock-gangster voice said, 'You're welcome, muthafucka.'

I said to Catfish, 'But we don't want any recruiting types sniffing about the place. Worse than the Beast.'

Later Catfish started drinking again, and he and Miguel got into a disagreement. Catfish drew a knife. Nobody moved. Then a voice called out. It was Blanchard. 'What happened to the tight ship, Swallow? What happened to discipline?'

I made some excuse, and Blanchard said, 'I'm not running a squat, is that clear?'

He walked away, his hands behind his back, past the pink string beans and juniper bush towards the glasshouses, where the latest brood of hybrids sweated – a consolation of sorts from our failed foray in the glades.

'Get him some coffee, for Christ sake,' I said about Catfish.

But the coffee didn't work. 'What have I done?' Catfish cried. I could sympathise. If I'd known what I'd been letting myself in for by signing up, I wouldn't have.

'What the fuck are we going to do with him?' Romeo asked.

I looked above me at the sky beginning to dusk.

'Let him stew.'

'I can't stand it. We'll take him out.'

I said, 'Are you crazy?'

Romeo put his hand under his friend's arm and hoisted him up and onto his unsteady feet.

'Come on,' he said, 'he can drink himself sober.'

We went to Deckards. As we entered, a couple of regulars raised their heads. It was all quiet. The stale smell of unwashed beer trays and spilled liquor filled the air. Underfoot was grime. Lola was behind the bar. 'What have you brought in, for Christ sake?'

'He needs a drink,' I said.

'That's the last thing he needs.'

'He's signed up to the military.'

Lola poured and we managed to get Catfish onto a barstool. Romeo held him so he wouldn't fall.

'He's having second thoughts,' Romeo said.

'No doubt,' Lola said. 'No fucking doubt.'

A woman walked in and sat opposite. We'd seen her there once before. Dressed in a yellow floral dress, she ordered a screwdriver. Then she took a mirror from her bag and looked at herself. She sighed, put the mirror away, took the wig from her head and lay it next to her. Her head was a patchy mix of tufted hair and baldness. Illness was written in her eyes. She started to comb her wig.

'Better without?' she asked us.

We agreed it was. She threw a few dollars on the bar, but Lola wouldn't take them. 'On the house.'

'Ah,' the woman said, 'you're feeling charitable.'

'My pleasure.'

The lady's name was Tara. She got up and sat next to Catfish. They whispered to one another, and for a time they left the bar. Romeo shook his head.

Lola said to Romeo, 'What is your friend thinking? The military will ship him overseas, he may not even make it back.'

'I know,' he said.

When they returned, Catfish was wearing Tara's wig. His lips were smeared with lipstick. She bought a round for everyone. This time Lola let her pay. Lola and Romeo seemed to have more to say to one another too. Before we left, I saw him reach around her while she stood at the jukebox. It looked like she liked that. I guess I'd have felt jealous, normally, but I didn't somehow. Someone else was on my mind. I let it be, drank my beer, and looked away.

Back at the Garden, Catfish was a long way from sober. He went to bed with his duffel bag clutched in his arms. At some stage the sergeant arrived. Catfish waved us all goodbye. He embraced Romeo, then came back to me and said, 'Goodbye muchacho.'

We settled back down to sleep, but not long after there was a knock on the barracks' door. It was Catfish again.

'Here,' he said, handing the duffel bag to me. 'Sergeant says I don't need this. Goodbye paradise.' He laughed, then turned dolefully and disappeared.

I opened his bag and looked inside. There was next to nothing in there. Underwear, socks, some shirts and a bible. The military had taken so much from me. At boot camp, they told me they were going to knock me down and build me back up again. But what they took away,

I never got back. I couldn't even tell you what that was anymore. I should've been outraged at watching someone else sign up, but I wasn't. I was just dog-tired. I zipped up the bag, threw it under my bunk, and went back to sleep.

That evening, Blanchard went away again.

'It's an emergency,' he said, throwing a small suitcase into his jeep. The bristle was dark about his jaw. His eyes were sleepless and agitated.

'She's upset,' he said, looking at the house, where Meribel stood by the doorway.

I watched her there, a glass in her hand.

'We were to do something together.'

The sun was setting. In the sky the clouds were dispersing. As the evening cooled, the skin on my face tightened.

Blanchard said, 'Can you watch her?'

'Watch her?'

'I mean go with her.'

'Where to?'

He sat into the jeep.

'To the theatre.'

He turned the key in the ignition, and the engine started up. 'She'll never forgive me,' he said, 'if she has to go alone.'

Meribel took a step further onto the porch. Blanchard lifted a hand in farewell.

'You'll be doing me a favour,' he said, giving his wife one last look. 'If this buyer bites, we could be saved.'

It was more ghost talk.

'And don't worry,' he added, 'I'll make it worth your while.'

He drove away. I never asked where to, or how he would make it worth my while. That night, I changed into the cleanest clothes I had, made my way to the house and knocked on the front door. Meribel answered and invited me inside. Nervously, I stepped across the threshold, but there was a calmness within the house which put me at my ease.

'He told you?' she asked.

'Sorry?'

'Blanchard; he told you to come with me to the theatre?'

'Yes,' I said.

She was already dressed for a night out – a black gown, high heels and a diamond necklace. She was smiling, and there was a giddy energy to her. In her hand was a drink. Her fingernails were painted a bright red. She blew on them and waved them through the air as she talked. The ice cubes in her glass tinkled.

'You should change,' she said.

When I hesitated, she suggested I wear something of Blanchard's.

'I don't know.'

'I insist,' she said, tilting her head and handing me her glass.

The alcohol – a gin and tonic – stung the back of my throat.

'Shower first,' she added, beckoning me up the stairs.

Briefly, I stumbled. Some gin spilled.

'Careful,' she said, then led me into the bathroom, and held her hand towards the shower. I kicked off my boots and pulled off my socks. The tiles were cool beneath my feet. I handed the glass back to her. She sipped from it. I had a strange feeling of trespassing again, that I shouldn't be here. It made something in my mind quiver.

Meribel said, 'I'll find you a suit while you shower.'

She looked at her watch while I stepped into the cubicle and turned on the water.

'There's a razor in there somewhere,' she said. 'You may as well shave.'

After I'd showered, I found the razor and scraped the beard from my face. When I'd finished, the door was open. I'd closed it before I went in. Had she been watching me? I stood before her with a towel wrapped round my waist. She reached out and touched my shaven cheek.

'Good,' she said.

She handed me a hanger with a cream linen suit and white shirt.

'Won't he mind?' I asked.

'Mind?' she laughed. 'He won't know.'

I took the hanger and waited for her to leave while I got dressed, but she didn't leave. She stayed standing where she was, regarding me.

I got dressed into Blanchard's clothes. Meribel watched. Then the doorbell rang. Meribel placed her glass on the bedside table and went downstairs.

I sat on the edge of the bed and looked in the mirror. Without the beard, I hardly recognised myself. I looked younger. 'Hello stranger,' I said. I finished dressing and emptied the glass of gin. My body hummed.

When I got downstairs, Meribel was waiting.

'You're like a new man,' she said.

The front door was open and the taxi waiting. I closed the door behind me and we took off for downtown. In the cab, I asked, 'what are we even going to?'

'A play,' Meribel said.

As we walked up the steps to the theatre, she linked her arm in mine. The reception was large. The carpet underfoot thick and luxurious. It had been a long time since I'd been anywhere like this.

Meribel walked directly to the bar and ordered for us both. Before she'd even taken a sip, her demeanour had changed. A dreaminess entered her eyes. Her pupils dilated and seemed to take in everything. She bought a programme and flicked through it carelessly before handing it to me. Then we were walking towards our seats, which were central to the balcony.

'How did he afford these tickets?' I asked.

'I think they were donated,' she said, 'by a buyer. I haven't been out in the longest time.'

The theatre went dark. The curtain was raised. The first actors made their entrance onto the stage: a man and woman. As the play progressed, there was a good deal of argument. There was tension. I didn't follow everything that went on. That wasn't because the play was bad, but because I was distracted by the darkness, the comfort and otherness of the space, and by Meribel.

At the interval, we went back to the bar. Meribel leant against me as I ordered, and we retreated to a table in the corner.

'What do you think?' she asked.

I told her I thought the play was good. She looked less convinced. We sat in silence and people-watched. The theatre was full of the well-dressed and the well-heeled, the coiffured and perfumed. I knew them. They were the type to come to a place like the Garden. I had served them, or people like them. Symbols of affluence were important to their class. The coveted flowers, their attire and attendance at a play – it all summed up an aspiration to be recognised as better-off, cultured, superior.

There was a part of me which hated these people, but I tried not to let that bitterness enter my blood. I was here, after all. I was letting myself dissolve into the scene, in order to imagine a different version of myself, of who I may have been or could become. I guessed art and plays helped you to escape the straitjacket of what people told you to be.

'The play reminds me of my life,' Meribel said to me as the bar filled with people.

'It does?'

'Desperately sad, isn't it?'

She was smiling. A smear of lipstick showed on her white teeth.

'I saw two lonely people living together,' I said.

'Yes,' she agreed. She cast her eyes down and looked into the glass. 'We're so ill-matched.'

She meant Blanchard. 'How did you meet?'

'I was his student.'

'You were?'

'He was a professor of botany.'

'And you were his best student?'

'No, I was not his best student. It all seems so long ago. A lifetime.'

'It can't have been? You're so young.'

She smiled. 'Of course, he likes to think he saved me.'

'From what?'

'Another life. Poverty, I guess. I don't know, myself maybe.'

There was a large mirror in a gilt frame at the other end of the room. I noticed how she looked at herself, repositioned her body, and took in her reflection. She saw me looking at her in the mirror, but it didn't stop her from gazing at herself. For a moment, I thought I saw Blanchard swimming in that sea of faces. Then she lowered her head as if she didn't want to be seen.

'I feel like a hostage at the Garden,' she said.

'But we're here,' I said. 'At the theatre.'

'By his request.'

'Did he also pick the play?'

'I did. You know I was an actress, once upon a time ... a student actress.'

'He saw you perform?' I asked.

'He did.'

'What was the play?' ,

'It was Shakespeare ... It doesn't really matter, does it? It was a bit part, a student production.'

'That can't have been so long ago?' I said.

'Are you trying to flatter me?'

'No, I meant ...'

Her head sank a little. 'You're so very serious, Swallow.'

The bell rang for the second half. I stood. I'd begun to feel uncomfortable. The shoes I wore, Blanchard's shoes, were too large, and the cuffs of my jacket, Blanchard's jacket, reached beyond my wrist. It made me think of Jamie, and how he'd wear my hand-me-downs.

'Let's cut,' she said.

'Really?'

She grabbed my arm and pulled me after her.

We pushed the doors open and found ourselves on the sidewalk. We were laughing. The air had cooled. What a relief that was. A police car cruised past – the Beast. Meribel leant against me. 'I don't want to go home,' she said, her breath warm on my neck.

'Won't he expect us to go back after the play?' I asked.

'Those were his instructions, but how will he know?'

'He'll ask us, won't he?'

'And we will lie.'

We were already walking down the street. Meribel was laughing again. She hailed a cab. Inside, she sat close to me, taking my arm in both her hands, lowering her head onto my shoulder. Then, in the darkness, she said, 'Those who love will be crucified. Those who do not are already dead.'

'What now?'

'It's from the play. Weren't you listening?'

'Where are we going?'

'I want to go to the reservation.'

I said I didn't think it a good idea, but Meribel insisted.

The driver wanted to know if she meant the casino, but she said no. He wanted more money if we were going onto the rez for no good reason. Meribel waved her hand as if it wasn't a problem, and so we drove on through the city to its outskirts. By the time we reached the rez, it was dark.

'I'm not sure this is a good idea,' I said.

'We're here now.'

But what did she want to do? And why here of all places?

'Can we simply drive?'

It might have been a limousine we were in, and she might have been some kind of royal personage, the way she gazed solemnly out the window. I asked her if being with Blanchard posed a problem. She looked at me innocently and asked me why.

'Because he's a racist.'

She said, 'He thinks I'm white.'

I looked at her in astonishment. Then she said, 'In the Caribbean, I'm what we call "red". He thinks I tan well.'

She said she was a little ashamed that she'd lost her accent. 'They think I turned my back on home.' Her father had moved to work in Florida, she said. Meribel had gone to college to study environmental science. Then her parents had split up. Her father died not long after, and her mother returned to Trinidad.

She said, 'We could run away together.'

I didn't like whatever game she was playing, and it wasn't clear whether she was serious or not. The deadpan delivery meant, I guess, I could take it any which way. The truth is I was scared of saying, 'Okay, let's run away', in case she laughed in my face, but I would have gone anywhere with her, at any time, and I guess that feeling had been growing over the months. I just hadn't a chance to show or tell her how I felt.

The pressure in the air was shifting. In the distance strange cloud contours were taking shape. The sky was fantastical, its colours changing from magenta to dark yellow. Part of me thought I was going out of my mind, as if we were existing on some foreign orb, living out the game-time of another species, playing our roles badly, with violent and careless glee.

She asked the driver to stop, and for what seemed like a long time we watched an old man walk a lame horse in circles about the escarpment. Then, as a full moon revealed itself, and shone brightly down on us, Meribel said, 'I think I've seen enough.'

When we got back to the Garden, and the taxi had left, we stood facing one another.

'He's not back for a few days,' she said quietly.

'And then we make our way into the swamp.'

'You're going back?'

'That's the plan.'

'I don't think that's a good idea.'

'He reckons it's the only way.'

'It's not. It's foolish, and dangerous. I wish you wouldn't go.'

'I've no choice.'

'But you do. You always have a choice, Swallow.'

She let out a sigh of impatience, then took my hand in her hers. I could have pulled away, but I didn't. I looked around. All was quiet. She guided my hand to her lips and brought me wordlessly into the house. We went into the hallway, up the stairs, and through to the bedroom, where she opened a window. A warm breeze billowed the curtain. She kept her gaze on me.

'What are we doing?' I said.

Without answering, she undressed. She stood before me naked, then slipped beneath the covers. I knew it was wrong. I knew it was a betrayal, but I followed her, shedding Blanchard's suit by the side of the bed, and kicking off his shoes.

'Are you sure?' I said.

She reached for me and I lay down beside her. Her body was warm and yielding. She breathed and groaned as I kissed her. From outside, on the barracks' deck, I could hear the sound of the hammock swinging back and forth on its rusty hinge. I didn't want people to hear us, so at times I covered her mouth with my hand. She kissed me, biting my lip until I felt my consciousness cloud with pleasure, and as she brought me inside of her, in my mind's eye, I saw an image of the ghost orchid unfolding with its otherworldly bloom.

Next day, Romeo and I drove to the dump. Romeo was pensive, mulling something over.

'What is it?' I asked.

'This load,' he said, 'it's a waste to throw it away. There are some worthwhile specimens. I don't understand?'

I sensed it wasn't the load he was mad about. He was upset that Catfish was gone. We were both hungover too; that never helps. Besides, I'd lied. 'We're not.'

He turned.

'Not what?'

'Not dumping.'

'Then what are we doing?'

'We're going to the rez.'

I turned the dial on the radio, landed on a feel-good spiritual station. The soft-speaking disc jockey talked of Jesus, and his ability to forgive. Romeo turned a medal on a chain he wore and blessed himself.

When we got there, Harper was edgy. 'Storm clouds,' he said, looking into the sky. But there were no storm clouds. It's true Harper was half-blind, but I knew he was talking about something else.

'He's speaking in riddles,' Romeo said. He threw a bag of compost before Harper.

'Hello, old timer,' I said.

'Good morning sunshine.'

'What's new?'

'What has been, will be again. Nothing new under the sun.'

'Ain't that the truth.'

I sat on a tree stump. Romeo found a crate.

'How's the boss?' Harper asked.

'He's a worried man,' I said.

Harper held a bromeliad in his hands. 'It'll be alright,' he said. 'The righteous will flourish.'

'Ask him about the orchid?' Romeo whispered.

I said to Harper, 'Can you bring us to the ghost?'

'The ghost?'

'You can guess.'

'Can I now?' Harper chuckled and shook his head. 'The day has finally come.'

'It's for Blanchard.'

'The Garden?'

'Right.'

'All is not right in paradise?'

'To say the least. You know what the hurricane did.'

'That I do.'

'And Blanchard needs it to stay afloat.'

Harper pointed into the distance. 'That's protected land you're talking about,' he said, 'with endangered species.'

'We tried once already. Had no luck,' Romeo said.

'Oh yeah?' Harper went about making tea.

'Logan,' I said.

Harper laughed. 'Hot-headed, wild – that boy. He should be given a new name!'

'You think?'

'Moon-struck.'

We laughed. 'You know his father's white. That's why people think he's so mean!'

We laughed some more, but Harper kept nodding, his eyes widening.

'Could be some truth in it,' I said.

Romeo stood and took down the last of the bags from the truck. He wiped his brow, then took out a cigarette and smoked. 'But you can show us. Isn't that right, hombre?' he said.

The old man looked up to Romeo. 'Me?'

Romeo took a step towards him. 'Sure,' he said. 'Blanchard said he'd pay you, arranged it all with Black Fox.' He looked about him. 'You know you look like you could use the money. Patch up the old shack.'

'I guess.'

Then Harper reached out and touched my hand.

'You're sure?' he said. I squeezed his hand, and he said, 'Okay then, so shall it be done.'

Pre-dawn, still dark, a few days later. Cool in the morning. Romeo – hard to wake. I shook him, and he pushed me away, mumbled something in Spanish, lost in a dream.

'Come on,' I said. 'Blanchard's waiting.'

He'd returned from his trip, upbeat and eager.

Romeo groaned at first, lifted himself to a sitting position, opened his eyes and looked at me. 'Today's the day,' he said, smiling, realising what we were setting out to do.

'Yes, it is.'

He rubbed the sleep from his eyes. With his shirt unbuttoned, and his boots untied, he walked with me to the house, slowly rousing himself by stretching his arms into the air and shaking out his hands. It was the way my brother used to wake, slowly, emerging from one world to another without urgency or haste.

Blanchard was packing a bag; he seemed slightly delirious and distracted in his excitement.

'Morning soldiers,' he said.

I didn't much like the military analogy, but I said nothing. Still, a beautiful morning was about to break.

You could feel it. The air was clean, and the outline of things was softened by the oncoming dawn. It was the kind of morning air that was free of the suffocating humidity which had beset us of late, the kind of morning you could take a breath of fresh air in, and think things were going to come good.

Meribel appeared from the house, her hair tied up and her arms crossed.

'There you all are,' she said. She made us coffee before we set off. She may not have approved of what we were doing, but she didn't try to stop us. 'Do you even know where you're going?' she said, handing the last of the coffee out.

'We've got an idea,' Blanchard answered.

'You'll need more than that, surely.'

'We have a guide.'

'A guide?'

'Harper.'

She took this in without objection. 'At least he knows his way around. You got everything you need?'

'I think so,' Blanchard said.

Romeo and I loaded the car with water and food, pillow cases for the flowers, beer, whiskey and a tent which Blanchard had insisted on, in case, he said, 'We need to make camp.'

'How long are you planning on going for?' Meribel asked bemusedly.

'Plan is we'll be back tonight. Some things are simply … contingencies.'

Meribel took a step towards her husband. 'Take care,' she said, kissing him on the cheek.

I might have turned away to let them have their moment of farewell, but I didn't, and I don't think Romeo did either. The affection between the two was strained. That was obvious. They'd been through a lot,

and were watching the dream they'd built together hang
by a thread.

Blanchard drove. There was a kind of mania in his eyes,
as if he were seeing something different to the rest of us.
The highways were almost empty, a fine mist rising from
the fields about us, and from the asphalt that shimmer of
morning heat that makes you think you're about to enter
a mirage.

I loved this time of day. The slate had been swept
clean from the day before and whatever had gone wrong.
Night-time thoughts were some ways off, and there
was the scent of promise in the morning, the sound of
possibility in the early rustlings amongst the cypress, and
even in the movements of those coming home; there was
the assurance of a new day, a new beginning, and with it
a kind of subliminal anthem that everything was going to
be alright.

Blanchard lit a cigar, and the truck filled with smoke.
The radio was turned up high. But as we got closer my
thoughts began to change. That new day feeling didn't last.
I imagined the snakes and gators of the glades. Gradually,
the good vibes gave way to a deep and hollow dread,
which found its way into the pit of my stomach. There
was no way out of it. We were on our way. Somewhere in
the swamp, at the end of our trip, would be the ghost. It
would all be worthwhile, I tried to persuade myself, but I
couldn't shake this new feeling of unease.

I checked one of the bags we'd packed for insect
repellent, took it out, sprayed it into my hands and
massaged my face with it.

'Give it here,' Romeo said. He too was excited.

I passed it to him, and he did the same as I'd done. We
cruised down the highway, light cresting the horizon, past
the twenty-four-hour shopping mall, gas stations and fast
food drive-thrus. I half closed my eyes, lending a shadowy

impression to the green gold landscape about us – glossing the telegraph poles and farm buildings, until there was less and less to see: a strip of road, and the watery mass of grasses on either side.

When we got to Harper's, he was standing in front of his shack leaning on a stick, a canoe laid out before him.

'He looks like he's been waiting all night,' Romeo said.

I let out a laugh, 'Like Noah, waiting for the waters to rise.'

'Is that a bow?' Romeo asked in wonder.

Sure enough, across Harper's back was slung a bow with a quiver of arrows.

'Old school,' I said.

Romeo said, 'Does he know what we're going for? Not a powwow, right?'

Blanchard killed the engine. We got out.

'Morning sunshine,' Harper said.

'Morning,' Blanchard said. Romeo and I took up the canoe and worked on tying it to the roof of the truck.

In Harper's hand was a map, which he unfurled on the bonnet of the truck. It looked old and much used.

'Can't we get there first,' Romeo said, tying the last of the knots to the canoe.

Harper looked up, his eyes rolling back in his head as if he were looking for something which was somewhere heavenward.

'Let him speak,' Blanchard said.

With a pencil Harper lightly traced our route south-west into the depths of the swamp.

'Is where we're going even on the map?' Romeo asked.

Blanchard barked, 'Hush now.'

Harper took no offence. His finger circled the parchment, and he said, 'That's a good enough question, you know.'

'How old is that map?' Romeo asked.

'Maybe fifty years?'

'Is it still accurate?' Blanchard wondered.

'Things have changed, sure,' Harper said. 'I've made notes and amendments.' He indicated the shading and shapes he had added in pencil.

Romeo started to chuckle. 'Some day, you'll need a new map.'

'Someday soon,' Harper agreed solemnly. 'The next map will look very different.'

'Where are we going?' Blanchard asked.

'There, that is where we are going.' Harper pointed to the south-west corner of the Fakahatchee.

Blanchard took a step back. 'God bless you, if you know how to get us there.'

'I do and I can,' Harper said.

'That's what I like to hear,' Blanchard said, but he looked less convinced than he sounded.

Harper kept circling with the pencil, spiralling inwards.

'What are you doing?' I said.

'It's how the glades are getting smaller, you see.'

The circle tightened about the contours of the map. 'We call this place a river of grass. And I fear it's dying.'

'Maybe we can hold off on the elegy until we're done,' Blanchard said, slapping the hood with his palm. But Harper wasn't done. A gust of wind blew the old map in his hand, but he held it firm.

'Don't get me wrong,' he said. 'This place is still wild. It's still untamed, but we ...' He struggled to find the right word, '... *encroach*. They dredge the sloughs too hard. The water is misdirected.'

Blanchard looked at him as if to say, 'What do you want me to do about it?'

'You know,' Harper said, 'I used to fish here as a youngster.'

'Oh Lord,' Blanchard said under his breath. His hand was on the door, ready to close it.

'Redfish, snook, spotted red trout – in abundance. Abundance. Now, I don't know.'

I looked at the map he had marked. None of it could capture his story.

'Let's get going before the day is gone,' Blanchard said.

Harper folded the map away and we got into the truck. We drove under an overpass, and over a bridge towards the glades as light was breaking. Light, still faint, but blossoming faster than any human thought, breaking the sleeping maw which had had us in its grip. Light which streamed across the Bay of Biscayne and greeted the pre-dawn workers of the Floridian plains. As we drove, light which gathered like an army now down the boulevards of the once blood-soaked streets of Ponce de León, light which had smuggled its way to Cuba, and back again on cargo-ships, and single-engine vehicles, and mocked the torchlight of night-time stowaways. Light which made its way into the Garden, where the men slept in the barracks in bunks made of pitch, and all around them, the house, and the breathing orchids, and beyond, where lone automobiles and police vehicles drove down the highways and interstates, where a coyote called out and was answered by the sound of its own voice, light.

Blanchard pulled the truck over and onto the side of a dirt road. There were grasses, pines and palms as far as the eye could see. Tree cover meant we were out of sight, in case the Beast came by. And there were sprigs, and dashes of colour, reds and whites, throughout the scene which was dense with vegetation and thick with the sound of animal life, carrying on about its business, oblivious for now to our human intrusion.

Romeo and I untied the canoe and threw our supplies into it. We drank a beer and started to make our way from the side of the road into the swamp. Harper first, followed by Blanchard, Romeo and I to the rear carrying the canoe.

And just like that we left one world and entered another, and as quickly a strange shiver went through me, as if something within my physical being knew this was a trespass of sorts. I'm sure we made a strange sight – a ragtag band of mercenaries, thrown together by the misaligned stars of fate. Pretty quickly I was out of breath; the air was thick with moisture. Sweat slid down my back and forehead, stung my eyes. We hiked through and over the mangrove. Romeo used a machete to cut his way through while Harper moved nimbly, seeming to know intuitively where and when to step.

'There.' Harper pointed in the direction we were to go, but to be honest, all I saw were more trees, more water, more danger. Through the canopy, wispy white clouds were reflected in the water. There was something tranquil about them, but the image was not to be trusted. All I could think was that clouds conceal danger. Harper waded farther and deeper, the sunlight glinting off the water's surface, shimmering, but beneath the surface of the water was darkness, and the rising smell was rank. Harper used his stick to lean on and push himself forward. With the dense foliage – palm, cypress and hardwood – the murk around us deepened.

I knew this place had been a dumping ground over the years. I knew we were walking on the watery graves of hundreds, if not thousands, of missing persons: men, women, slaves and convicts. The water was made of sunlight and blood. It entered my boots and rose up my leg – warm and wet and deadening.

'I don't know if I'm more afraid of snakes or gators,' Romeo said, helping me navigate the canoe through the water.

Blanchard laughed out loud.

'What's so funny?' Romeo wanted to know.

'One will bite,' Blanchard said, 'the other will drown you, tear you to pieces, and eat you.'

He laughed some more.

'Okay, I get it,' Romeo said. Then he looked at me, all bug-eyed, and said 'asshole' under his breath. 'When do we get in this thing?' he said, pushing the canoe. I told him a little further on, once the water got deeper.

'Which way now, Harper?' Blanchard said.

Harper pointed to a roseate spoonbill feeding, and we stopped to watch it briefly. Its white neck was like a bar of light, and there was a streak of red across its plumage that looked like dripping blood.

We pushed on. Underfoot was quicksand. With each step it was like the ground was about to give way. It made us hurry, even though I knew we needed to take our time and be careful. Pretty soon, the water was up to our chests. I can't say I felt any better than Romeo. He hung back. The mosquitos were everywhere, small dark clouds of them, buzzing and biting.

'Come on,' I called out to Romeo. 'We need you too. Don't want to lose out on the glory, do you?'

He grunted. 'What's the expression you have in English,' he said, pointing to Harper, 'the blind leading the blind.'

'I believe that's the one you're looking for,' I said.

He laughed a frantic laugh, a yelp more like it, and heaved himself through the water. I thought of his near-drowning experience on the beach, and imagined how much more afraid he must have been than me. I stepped nervously, my footing unsure, sinking and wary of each and every next step. And though it held obvious dangers, it felt good. I was happy for some stupid reason I couldn't name. Maybe it was as simple as being out of the Garden.

Maybe it was the excitement of actually taking a risk outside of its confines. It was something like the military, like war. But this was not war, I had to remind myself. War leaves an indelible stain on the soul, and no amount of drinking, of abnegation, or of getting lost can wipe away that black mark. Not even the most beautiful and precious thing I'd found beneath this ungodly firmament could clean the slate.

'We're all going to die,' war whispers into your ear when you are about to fall asleep, then when you wake, it shouts it in your face. It doesn't ever let you forget.

But this was something else, a different kind of struggle with an obsession which had been Blanchard's, but which had also become my own. And that was how and why I found myself in a swamp looking for the ghost orchid, chest-deep in warm, soupy water, lilies in view, a nighthawk's screech in the air, and a sense of coming to, of being lost enough to find myself.

I stopped to take a breath, noticed a spider making its way along a branch above me. Fig and pond apple trees surrounded us. It gave me pause. For Blanchard, the ghost meant survival. It meant he could rebuild and fulfil the ambition and promise he had for his and Meribel's life together. For so long, they had nurtured orchids and the orchids in turn had given back and provided them with a livelihood. But now the scales were tipped, and Blanchard needed the rarest of orchids. Already I was beginning to wonder whether it would be enough; it might be to save the Garden, but what of Meribel and Blanchard, of their marriage, and what of Meribel and me?

I guess the ghost had started to haunt us all in various different ways, and had come to embody a whole host of associations which for me meant the past and my brother Jamie in particular. Imagine it, a flower so elusive and mysterious that it contained all you ever yearned for, and all you couldn't have. That the ghost existed deep inside the swamp meant risk, treachery and possible death, but also – if somehow you had luck enough on your side – life, survival, redemption. A symbol of contradictory impulses then, held in the wispy effervescence of a flower which seemed to float on air.

The murky water lapped against my chest. I saw what I thought was poison ivy, but surely that was the least of our worries, for who knew what beasts swam beneath the water's filmy surface? I knew – alligators. Prehistoric fucking animals – they might as well have been dinosaurs. Deadly, stealthy, famished killers. Every perturbation in the air suggested their presence, every dark shadow, every ripple of water I knew could be them.

We waded and waded, farther and farther from civilisation, before we came to anything.

'Are you sure about this?' Romeo said.

'He can't swim,' I said to Blanchard.

'Let's hope,' he said, 'there'll be no need.'

Romeo looked petrified.

'The eyes,' Blanchard said raising the stick in his hands. 'Poke them in the eyes, if they go for you.'

We floundered on. It was a beautiful place, more garden than the Garden itself, more pure and real, untouched and natural, but that didn't make it any less dangerous.

'We're not far,' Harper said, ploughing on. He pointed to what looked like a small islet, a hammock, covered in cordgrass, saw palmettoes and cabbage palms. A ridge of limestone jutted out. As Harper pointed, something slid into the water ahead of us.

Romeo put his end of the canoe down, and I let mine drop into the water. He stopped and stood very still. He turned then and started backing away.

'This is crazy,' he said.

'It's only a baby,' Harper said. 'It'll leave us be.'

'Come on,' Blanchard encouraged. He climbed into the canoe and asked Romeo to pull him. He tied his red bandana about his head, and beneath his hat he looked like some white king in the jungle.

Harper said, 'It won't attack unless you provoke it.'

I had no way of knowing if what Harper said was true or not. 'Harper,' I said, 'are you sure?'

'Mating season is over,' he said confidently.

My foot got caught on something and I froze. I thought it might have been a gator, but nothing happened. I removed my foot carefully and kept on. My heart hurt in my chest, it beat so hard and fast, and my mouth was dry with the taste of swamp.

'The ghost is on that hammock,' Harper said.

He made it there first and pulled himself up onto the bank. He stood and swatted the flurry of buzzing mosquitos about him. I picked up the pace. As I neared the bank, I felt something sinewy brush against my leg. I kept going. Further on, a rigid mass more solid and unyielding came against me. It had the force of something indomitable, ancient and alive. I sensed it taking in my being, weighing up the threat. I froze, braced myself for an attack, waited for the bite and death roll, but it didn't come. I let out a breath, kept moving, pulled myself up onto the muddy bank and reached out. Harper took my arm and heaved me up.

'Was that a snake?'

'Can't be sure,' I said, though I knew it wasn't.

I don't know if he'd seen my scare with whatever it was below the water, but Romeo was looking more and more nervous. He held onto the canoe and began to clamber aboard.

'Careful,' Blanchard called out.

Then he stood up in the canoe in order to help Romeo. This was probably the worst thing he could have done. The canoe wobbled back and forth.

'He shouldn't have done that,' Harper said, looking on.

Romeo held out his hand, but as he did so, a gator rose up out of the water with almost supernatural stealth. This was not the baby. This was its mother. Its jaws opened for Romeo, but Blanchard managed to haul him onto the canoe.

'Holy fuck,' Romeo exclaimed; whichever way the canoe had been rocked, and the water disturbed, he fell back. Blanchard turned and stood. He stumbled, and with their combined weights and ungainly movement, the canoe capsized.

The gator rose again. This time it got a hold of Romeo, and with one fierce strike it took the man in its jaws and turned him in the water, rolling him one time, and then another, into a coiling vice grip.

Blanchard made his way to the bank. From where we were, Harper swung his bow into his hands, loaded an arrow, aimed and fired. It plunged into the water but did not connect. Then, lightning fast, he fired another, and then another. At least one arrow hit the gator, but who knows if it managed to penetrate anything other than the thick wall of reptilian hide. I expected to hear Romeo howl, and scream, but all I heard was the splashing thunder of swamp water. With his final arrow, Harper hit the gator in the eye, and the animal relinquished its grasp of Romeo, sinking back into the murky depths once more.

Romeo emerged from the water, his arm in the air as if he were waving, and in his eyes was the look of a man who had accepted his fate, steely, resigned, fierce, as if sunlight had lanced his very pupils. The water went quiet and calm. Sunlight returned to its surface.

Romeo turned the canoe over with his one good arm and climbed back in. He surveyed the water around him. It was dark and blood-curdled. The gator was gone, but some of our bags and supplies floated away; the tent, the bottles of beer, a satchel.

There followed an eerie stillness. Romeo paddled the boat back to the hammock as best he could. I helped him onto the islet and Blanchard pulled the canoe off the water.

'Jesus,' Romeo said.

I put my arm about him. He was shook and stunned, but worse than that, he was bleeding heavily.

'I guess he's not as blind as we thought,' Romeo said of Harper. Blanchard reached into his jacket and came out with a bottle. He unscrewed the cap and gave the whiskey to Romeo.

'Drink it,' he said.

Romeo did as he was told. 'Thank you.'

'Staunch the puncture wounds and you'll be fine.'

His arm had been pierced four or five times. Shredded but unbroken, by the looks of it. I ripped my shirt, bandaged the wounds and made a sling for his arm.

'We have to keep on,' Blanchard said.

Romeo's face was ashen, his eyes wet. 'I can't,' he said.

Blanchard put a hand on his shoulder, and whispered, 'We've no choice.'

Harper turned. I kept my arm about Romeo and we followed the Seminole, making our way through the thickets, the brush and sedge with a greater sense of urgency. Harper seemed to know where he was going, but then he'd stop, and raise his head to the bromeliads above as if looking for a clue, or inspiration, or God knows what, before moving quickly on. How his milky eyes knew where to take us, I do not know.

Romeo struggled. After a short time, we came to a clearing where a pop ash stood. I asked Harper how he knew where the ghost was, and he answered by saying he'd known about it for a long time, which didn't really answer my question, but I was used to that with Harper.

When we came to the tree, Blanchard said, 'where?' Harper pointed upwards. I looked. All I saw was a pocket of endless sky.

'Up there,' Harper said, 'at the top of that tree.'

'How are we supposed to get up there?' Blanchard said.

Harper took a rope from around his waist and handed it to me.

'Not me?'

'Yes,' Harper said.

'I've never climbed a tree that high.' The rope lay limp in my hands.

'First time for everything.'

Blanchard helped tie the rope about my waist and lifted me onto the first branch.

'It should be close to the top,' Harper said. 'Look carefully.' He handed me a pillowcase. 'Then put it in this.'

I stood back. The tree was tall and sturdy.

'How do you know it's up there?'

'It is,' he said, and as I made my way upwards, he shouted, 'don't look down.'

The branches made a haphazard ladder; I took one step after another. Pretty soon my arms and legs began to ache with the effort. Still, I made steady progress. I could hear them talking down below. Every so often, they shouted up some encouragement.

'There you go.'

'Higher.'

'Nearly there.'

Halfway up, I stopped. My mouth was dry. I had no water. Beer and whiskey do nothing for the thirst. Foolish, I thought. I looked down. That was a mistake. Everything wavered below me. The men looked tiny, a million miles off.

'Don't look down,' Harper called out.

Too late. The forest seemed to spin about me. An egret swooped and made me lose my footing. I slipped and caught onto the branch below.

'Use the fucking rope,' Blanchard hollered.

I tied a knot onto the branch above me, and went that way for a while, branch to branch, but it was taking so long I left it, and thought if I didn't get up there soon I'd lose my nerve. I kept on, and pretty soon I was close to the top, about forty feet in the air. I looked closely from one branch to the next but saw nothing.

'The body of the tree,' Harper shouted. 'Not the branch.'

His voice was faint, like an echo in a well. I searched the trunk, up and down, and began to think I'd be making the descent empty-handed, when I saw it. It didn't look attached to the body of the tree at all, as if the flower was floating in thin air. Its roots barely discernible, like faint veins of light clinging onto the tree. It was smaller than I had imagined, and there was something winsome, something fragile about it. As I gazed at the ghost, it felt as though I was being placed under the most mysterious of spells.

'Cut it free,' Harper called up.

I took the knife from my belt and cut the flower from the trunk. I held it in my hand and looked at it. Strange, but it felt like it was giving me something supernatural – a kind of access to something from the past. I imagined its fleshy petals reaching out like the long and elegant fingers of my mother, and even in the swampy heat, the sweat gathering behind my neck and down my back, I shivered and felt, if not saved, vindicated somehow – that the journey had after all been worth it.

I placed the ghost into the pillowcase Harper had given me, then shoved that under my shirt. It was a crude way to treat such a delicate thing, but I couldn't think of any other way, bar throwing it down, and who knew what would happen if I did that. I climbed from one branch to another. The rope was getting in my way, so I untied it and threw it downward; it caught on a branch and stayed there. I looked down and saw Romeo, Harper and Blanchard looking up. I hugged the tree and slid down, swiftly, and a little recklessly. Maybe it was the ghost, but I felt unassailable. I let go of the last branch and dropped, the sweat spilling from my face, gasping, out of breath and parched.

'Give it here,' Blanchard said.

I dug into my shirt, found the pillowcase and said, 'something to drink.'

He handed me the bottle of whiskey, took the pillowcase and opened it. He removed the ghost, held it up to the light, and let out a gasp.

'This one small thing is going to change everything,' he said.

'It already has,' I said, pouring water over my hands.

And then the cypress around us seemed to close in. I heard something making its way through the undergrowth. It was impossible to know what it was. I'd heard of wild panthers pacing the swamps, stalking their prey. I looked into the thickets, and saw nothing but the massy green density, humming and buzzing.

'It's not just the water we need to be wary of,' Blanchard said.

'It's as dangerous as anywhere else,' Harper said.

I guess he was right in his way.

Then Romeo threw up.

'We need to get him to a doctor,' I said.

He groaned some, and Harper said, 'It'll be okay.'

But Romeo's hands were shaking, and the blood had drained from his face. The shock he'd experienced meant he couldn't celebrate the ghost. Its attainment had been tainted now. My own responses were delayed; seeing the gator attack had set a host of chemicals coursing through my blood – adrenaline, and whatever else. I felt sick, spent.

'Sit,' Harper said. 'Calm yourself.'

Blanchard rooted for more whiskey, handed it to me and told me to drink.

'Better?'

'Yeah,' I said. 'Thanks.'

I took another sup. I could have emptied the bottle.

'We need to get the orchid back to the lab,' Blanchard said.

'And the gators?'

'Tread careful,' Harper said.

I reached for the bottle again. The alcohol burned my throat and left me light-headed. Romeo looked dazed. I handed the bottle to him, and he drank.

'Okay, brother?'

'Yeah,' he said, 'I'll be okay.'

'Jump in,' I said. 'I'll be your guide.' Again, it was that invincible thing; having taken the orchid, I felt golden. Romeo sat into the canoe, and we started back out across the swamp, through the blood-soaked water with the gators and the snakes. My fear was gone. We had the ghost, and that was all that mattered.

There was a certain nervous euphoria on our return journey. Blanchard was loud, probably drunk, talking like some victorious invader of old. Sure, it was tempered by Romeo's injuries, but that didn't stop him talking like a madman.

'Men, you did well. I'm proud of you. I am. We met adversity, but we didn't let it stop us. We have what we came for.'

He placed his hand on my shoulder as he drove. I looked back to Romeo. He was looking out the window wondering, I'm sure, what on earth he had gotten himself involved in. I guess we all were in our own ways.

When we dropped Harper off, he said, 'You take good care. And mind that bloom. It needs some care. And Romeo, too.'

At the Garden, Meribel had been in one of the greenhouses. She came out when she heard the truck. Blanchard had blown the horn, and I held my hand out the window and waved.

'You survived,' she said when we'd gotten out of the vehicle.

'We didn't just survive,' Blanchard said. 'We conquered.'

She smiled. She looked relieved, but Blanchard wanted something else. He wanted more of a response, he wanted adulation. He held out his hands.

'Do you know what this means?'

Meribel ignored his grandstanding and attended to Romeo. She inspected the bandage and wound. The puncture marks hadn't stopped bleeding. They were deep, and ragged, and the flesh about them had swelled. It was not a clean bite, but a dirty mess, as if the arm had been slashed by knives.

'What happened?' she said to Blanchard.

'Gator attack.'

'Jesus.'

'He'll be fine.'

'I'll bring him to A&E.'

Meribel shook her head and walked with Romeo to the jeep to take him to the hospital as Blanchard and I brought the pillowcase of flowers into the lab.

'Careful,' Blanchard commanded.

He removed each specimen, holding the ghost orchid delicately in his hands before transporting it to its special chamber.

It looked so brittle, the ghost of a flower. 'Will it survive?' I asked.

I guess that's not what Blanchard wanted to hear. He grunted.

'We need Romeo back as quickly as possible,' I said.

'That we do,' he said.

'If he's not fit to work, the whole escapade will have been for nothing.'

Blanchard turned, and held me firmly in his gaze.

'Escapade,' he said in disgust. 'You don't think I fucking know that, Swallow?'

I swept, then smoked. Blanchard prepared the lab, and the chamber, his movements laboured and agonised. I watched him observe the orchid with an earnestness which seemed to border on reverence. Then I heard a plane above, but nothing of it was visible in the sky, just the sound of its far-off engine, and the hum of a machine at work.

When Romeo returned he was re-bandaged and a little high from whatever painkillers they had given him.

'You okay?' I said when I saw him. He looked pale and tired.

He nodded. 'They took good care of me.' He shook the bottle of painkillers in his bandaged hand.

'Time for you to do your magic,' Blanchard said.

'It's science not magic,' Romeo said, and smiled weakly. 'It's about light and temperature.'

He went to work steadily, concentrating hard on the job at hand. After a while, Blanchard and I retreated. We were of no help to Romeo's expertise. I watched Blanchard slink back to his house with his head bowed, his triumphalism from earlier in the day replaced by a kind of weary resignation.

In the days that followed, I laid low. Did odd jobs, safe things as I saw them, cutting wood, sweeping, digging the irrigation trenches. I stayed away from downtown, avoided the Beast and kept to the Garden until I almost felt like I wasn't needed. It was all about the ghost and Romeo now. When I went drinking, I went alone. It was later that week when I pulled into the strip mall with the Chinese restaurant, and nail salon, I felt the queer déjà vu which seemed to shadow my life. It was the kind of feeling that had followed me about one year after another, as if it was all the same year, the same book, the same broken, tripping record, the stylus hopping beneath my brother's hand, or was that mine?

I stood outside Deckards, or what had been Deckards. It was gone, had been burned to the ground. The sight of its scorched shell left a dull ache inside me. I got out of the car to broken glass and the acrid smell of smoke. Inside of what had been the bar I could see the charred pleather seats, a smashed mirror.

I stood outside the ruins, barely able to move. I thought about Lola, and a deep sadness filled me until I thought I couldn't take it anymore. I closed my eyes and dropped to my knees. When I opened them again, I saw a man walking through the scorched debris. He was dressed in rags, his hair and beard white. I don't know what he was looking for. I didn't ask. Instead, I picked up a photo from the remains. It was of Lola. Its edges were singed, and faded, but there she was, smiling back at me with her hands on her hips. I felt the strangest sorrow, then folded the photo and put it in my pocket.

'What happened?' I said to the other man, but he didn't answer. He was mumbling to himself. 'Oh Lordy,' he said. His head remained lowered and he kept searching for whatever he was looking for. I started looking too, then stopped, not knowing what I was doing. Whatever it was he was looking for, I can't imagine he ever found it.

Afterwards, I drove to Lola's. The gate to the complex was stuck. I looked to where the CCTV camera was, pulled my hood up and pushed the gate open. I knocked on her door but there was no answer. A neighbour arrived. I asked her had she seen Lola. She shrugged and answered in Spanish that she hadn't. She said something else I didn't understand. Something quick, and colloquial, and unconcerned. She raised her eyebrows and pointed beyond the pool to where the office was.

Some children were in the playground. I don't know why they weren't at school. An old woman watched me. Did she know Lola, I asked. I wasn't sure the woman understood me or cared. She never answered. For a moment, I wondered, was Lola even her real name? Or was it simply the name over all these years that she had given me. That she was perhaps known to her neighbours as someone else.

A man stood in the pool, submerged to his chest. He wore dark sunglasses. I could tell he was watching me. I had never seen him before, and I didn't know who he was. I went to the reception. I rang a bell. A Chinese woman emerged. She didn't speak English. She made a phone call and a man appeared. I asked about Lola. And he said, 'No Lola. No here.'

I asked him who lived in no. 9. His answer was consistent.

'No Lola,' he said.

I went back to no. 9 and banged on the door. I walked down the steps and tried to peer through the windows. I saw nothing. No one was there. As I was leaving, a boy with a bandana tied over his head threw his cigarette to the ground. I asked him had he seen Lola. He pointed into the distance, where the sun was setting. The sky was turning into a spectacular burnished bronze. I was going to ask the boy another question, but a man, it could have been his father or uncle, placed himself in front of the boy. In Spanish, he spoke sharply to the boy with the kind of bravado I knew from experience could end in violence.

I left and drove back to the Garden. When I got there, Romeo was in the lab.

'Hombre,' he said looking at me quizzically. 'What's wrong?'

I told him the bar was gone.

'Deckards?'

'Burned down.'

Romeo shook his head.

'What happened?'

'Who knows?' I said.

He kept working. The ghost orchid was before him inside its special chamber.

'The temperatures?' I said.

'Are all correct.'

He had a small knife in his hands. Stem cuttings lay in paper towels before him. I imagined taking the knife into my hands. I don't know what I might have done. It felt like a black dye had spread through my brain, and for a moment, my mind was a blank. I went outside and took up the axe. I chopped wood until I couldn't.

Then, I walked back to the barracks and fell into the hammock. Blisters blossomed on my palms, and the stars above me spun.

I slept, then woke in darkness. I felt boxed in, needed to get out. My mouth was dry. I drank water, forwent coffee and took the keys for the truck.

I drove for what felt like a long time. From one highway to another, through the city, across its bridges and overpasses. My arms became heavy and tired, my back tense. The flatness of the landscape stretched before me.

I stopped for one drink, then another. I got coffee from a gas station, made a U-turn in the parking lot. I stopped again. It was another bar. It looked like every other, had the smell of stale beer and detergent. I got talking to a man. I can't remember what about exactly. It was good-natured banter, but we were both more interested in drinking than getting to know one another. Closing time came, last orders.

'Back to mine for a nightcap?' he said.

'Sure,' I said.

I followed him through a maze of streets to an apartment. Inside was warm. He sat me down at a table and went to fetch some beer. The light from the refrigerator spilled out in the space and cast the man in shadow.

We talked some more. Then he said, 'From Ireland? I've never had the pleasure. I'm a born and bred Floridian. I don't think I'm ever gonna leave. There's something about the sunshine and the swamp that keeps me close to God.'

'God?' I said nervously.

'Sure. You're not a God-fearing man?'

I didn't answer.

'Listen to me now. Out here we're on the tip of the world, right? We don't really even have the right to be living here what with all the swamp water and animals and shit. Still, this is God's country. He wanted us to be right here when there's no other good reason for humankind to be able to exist out here. You follow? You understand?'

I nodded and sipped my beer.

'Look around you, sure you see fast food joints, highways, malls, residential units, but that's just the façade. Behind all that there's life, there's a wildness and the closer we can get to that the closer we can be to God.'

He paused. What followed was an unnerving silence between us. For a moment, in the half-light, I thought he was holding out his hand to me, and was about to say, 'Let's pray', or something. Maybe he was a Baptist, like the mother and daughter I once met on my way through Texas some years previous who had wanted to pray together with me.

'I don't know,' I said, disturbing the stillness.

'What don't you know, friend?'

'If there is a God would he have unleashed the hurricane which caused so much destruction and death?'

He pushed back his chair and laid his hands on the table. 'Did I say he was a *loving* God?'

Again, I had no answer, though he had asked the question with such ferocity, I felt like I'd disappointed him.

'Well did I?'

'No,' I said.

He exhaled.

I had passed the test, it seemed, for now.

'No,' he said. 'I did not say He was a *loving* God.'

'You think …?'

He drank from his beer, wiped his mouth with his sleeve and said, 'I don't think it. I know that He is *not* a loving God.'

He let that settle in, then got up to get us another beer.

On his way back, he said, 'He is a wrathful God, but we still need to seek Him out, we still need to get as close as we can.'

I took the bottle from him and raised it as if I were toasting what he was saying.

'God hates sin but loves the sinner; we need not be afraid.'

'No?' I said.

'For even though I walk through the valley of the shadow of death, I will fear no evil.'

I sensed a certain fault in the man's line of reasoning here, but the beer was good, so I kept my mouth shut. He was standing now, gesticulating and, I guess the word is, *preaching*.

At some stage during his sermon, I think we had got on to the devil's work and such, a door opened. A woman appeared. She approached the table we were sitting at. She wore a long T-shirt, and she looked like she'd been asleep, and that we'd woken her. She didn't look happy at all, in other words.

'Who the fuck is this?' she said.

The man stuttered. His tone changed. 'This is my good friend …'

He didn't know my name. I didn't know his.

'Get no-name the fuck out of here, you fucking asshole.'

I stood up. On the windowsill, I noticed a supermarket-sold orchid in a pot. 'You have an orchid,' I said, pointing with some surprise.

'Fucking thing never flowers,' the man said.

'And you're a fucking asshole too,' the woman said to me. 'Mr fucking no-name.'

The man kind of froze then. It was like he was playing a game of moving statues. I left. But the woman's voice was ringing in my ears. I didn't know where I was. Eventually, I found my way back to the bar where the truck was. I got in and, for a time, I drove, without a thought in my head. I drove from one street to the next until I found the highway. I made my way to the back roads I knew. The lights of the city blurred in my line of vision. I was so tired and tight I didn't know if I was going to make it. Then, in the distance, I saw fires burning.

When I passed what I thought was one bonfire, and then another, I realised that cars had been set alight. Groups had gathered. This was on the side of the road leading out of the city. There was black smoke billowing. There were the sounds of chants and songs, cheers and weeping.

I stopped, rolled down the window. A boy approached.

'You don't wanna get out, mister,' he said. 'Better you keep on.'

I did as the youngster said. I drove faster, and more recklessly, as if my life depended on it. For miles to see, and all over the United States, for all I knew, a fire was spreading, and with it a gathering mob. I kept driving, didn't stop. I passed a fogging truck off Krome Avenue and drove through the chemical mist. When I found my way to the dark corner where the Garden was, I felt a disappointed relief.

The lights of the main house were out. Miguel stood on the porch with a weapon cradled in his hands.

He wasn't a big man, never had been. Now he looked dwarfed by the semi-automatic slung across his shoulders like a toy. But it wasn't a toy. There was a nervous grin on his face. His gaze dropped to the weapon in his hands. His lips twitched. Before I got out of the truck, I felt the vertigo of the drive. I was afraid to open the door in case the ground I placed my feet onto was still moving.

Miguel stood tall, and I got out. We didn't speak. He held his shoulders back and raised the semi in his hands as if to say: look at this. Look at me.

'Noches,' he said.

I said, 'Don't point that fucking thing at me.'

He laughed. I shook my head and walked. This then, was the new regime. A security measure that Blanchard had insisted on, no doubt. I'd seen it coming, so I wasn't surprised. I noticed there was a light on at the back of the main house: Blanchard's office. I looked to the lab. It was dimly lit, but inside I could see a figure moving. It was Romeo.

I made no move, neither towards the house nor Blanchard's office. All I wanted to do was fall into bed, but I went to the lab. I needed to see the ghost. The door was open, and I let myself in. In the dim light, Romeo was busy at work.

'Where were you?'

His tone was desperate. He looked as tired as I felt, as if he hadn't slept, his eyes wide, and a little crazed.

'I had some business to take care of ...' My voice – the voice that came from me – was angered. I heard it at a distance from my body, as if someone else had delivered the words.

He shook his head, placed the trowel and plant down.

'You shouldn't have left.'

In the lamplight, everything seemed to waver. A moth fluttered. Romeo took a deep breath. He lowered his voice. 'Something's happened,' he said.

I felt his breathing. I heard my own.

'What?'

Romeo's figure flitted in the dusky light.

'Logan,' he said, 'from the rez.'

'What about him?'

'He came here.'

'What did he want?'

'He said he was here to make a delivery.'

Outside, a mockingbird rasped in the undergrowth. In the distance, I thought I could hear the sound of children's voices, but no, that was impossible.

'A delivery?' I said.

'He was raving.'

'Where is it?'

'Outside.'

I put my hand on the handle of the lab door and swung it open. Romeo followed me out. What happened next felt like a dream. We went out to where Miguel stood guard. Then we walked to the side of the house where another truck was parked. Without saying a word, Romeo pointed to the cargo bed. Mosquitos whined and swarmed. The darkness thickened. I went to the tarpaulin and pulled it open.

There was Harper, his lifeless body.

A fearful shudder shook me. My hands began to tremble. No, I thought. Not Harper. I managed to say, 'What happened?'

'He was dead when he got here.'

'Dead?' I said, not believing it.

He nodded. 'Delivered like that.'

'You mean dumped?'

'I moved him,' Romeo said, 'from the ground to here.' He pointed to the cargo bed. 'I thought it would be better.'

'He didn't need to kill him.'

'I guess Logan didn't want Harper bringing us to the ghost.'

'He heard?'

'He must have.'

The night sky seemed to shrink and vanish into the pupil of his eyes. Petty, I thought, the grudges of prideful men. Too petty. And death — the badge of their dishonourable hearts.

I looked to the corpse. There remained the trace of a smile on Harper's face, but his mouth was smeared with dried blood which was blackening with every passing second. Already some flies had congregated about his cracked and fulsome lips. I swatted them away. 'God damn it,' I said.

More startling and sickening was the wound which made its way about his neck like a jagged incarnadine necklace of his own mortality. Some awful reckless feeling rose up within me, and this time I wanted to let it loose.

'What does Blanchard want us to do?'

'To dispose of the body ...' Romeo said, holding his hands out.

I leaned over Harper and pulled the dog tags from his neck. I closed his heavy, milky eyes. Then I got into the truck, and Romeo followed. He threw me the keys, and I sat there for what seemed an eternity, before driving back into the blackest night to bury the body of my friend.

We drove to a disused quarry. The road to it was cracked, and I was afraid we'd puncture or break down. The trees about us moved in the darkness – like subdued witnesses – and a part of me thought that was only right. The quarry itself was full of echoes. Trucks and machinery stood like rusted silent sentinels in the gloom. Below I heard something scurry in the dark.

'I can't do it,' I said. 'I can't leave him like this.'

Romeo stood in the darkness, and said, 'If we don't … we all go down.'

'Really? You believe that? Is that something Blanchard said to you?'

'I don't know. Makes sense.'

'Nothing makes sense.'

'No,' he said.

'It never did.'

We shared a cigarette. It felt like the shadows were circling us – creatures, and spirits, we could not see. What meant harm, and what did not, I couldn't figure. All I knew is we were not alone.

'He needs to be buried with his people,' I said. 'He deserves at least that.'

'Yeah,' Romeo said. 'If it was me …'

He didn't finish what he was going to say, if he knew what he was going to say at all. The moon revealed itself, stern mistress of the tongue-tied and inarticulate. It was late into the night, close to dawn, and it was all something of a blur. We took a chance and went to where Black Fox lived on the rez. I knocked on his door, and a woman answered. I asked for him and he came and stepped outside.

'What are you doing here?'

'I need your help.'

'What is it?'

'It's Harper …'

'What about him?'

I told him he'd been killed.

'You take a big risk coming here,' he said.

'His body was delivered to the Garden …'

We stepped further from the house. Black Fox said, 'Tell me what happened.'

I told him Romeo had said Logan dropped the body.

'Logan?'

'I'm not here for recriminations. I'm here to bury Harper.'

'He was one of us,' Black Fox said, which was true, I guess, except that Harper had been ostracised in his way. He was a black Native American, and he'd been essentially pushed to the edges of the reservation.

'What do we do?'

'Logan, damn it,' Black Fox said. He raised his head heavenward.

'Is there a native plot or do we bring him to his house and burn it?'

He looked at me as if I was crazy. 'Burn his house?'

'You tell me.'

'You've been watching too many movies, white man.'

But what we ended up doing was stranger still.

'He's got no family,' Black Fox said. 'We'll take him to the glades, see him off in the place he loved.'

Then he asked me where Harper was, and Romeo got out of the truck and pointed to the cargo bay. Black Fox uncovered the tarpaulin and took in the body.

'Come,' he said then, and we went to the back of his house and together we pulled a canoe onto the truck. Black Fox went to retrieve a red gasoline container and handed it to Romeo.

'Blanchard knows?' he said.

'He wanted us to dispose of the body,' Romeo said.

'But not to call the Beast?'

'No.'

'That's good.'

We took off. Romeo in the back. Black Fox rode shotgun. The sound of the gasoline slushing back and forth in the container made me uneasy. I imagined the truck crashing and all of us going up in a ball of flames. Part of me would have been okay with that. The wet prairie lay ahead of us, dark and stirring, on the verge of waking up, or imploding. Who knew?

'What about Logan?' I said.

'Let us deal with him.'

'You'll turn him in?'

Black Fox said nothing.

'Or punish him?' Romeo asked.

'We'll deal with him,' he said.

He shook his head and turned. I got the impression he had to deal with a lifetime of grief from his nephew. When we got to the glades it wasn't far from the estuary where we'd found the ghost.

'Here,' Black Fox said.

The sun was rising. I had mixed feelings about that. How do you consecrate a murder? In darkness, I thought, but this man's life had been lived in daylight and hope. We stopped, got out. Black Fox pulled the canoe from the truck and onto the water – innocent vessel. A black-beaked ibis waded by, oblivious to our presence in the sawgrass. Then we took Harper's body from the truck. Oh Lord, what a load he was. Black Fox held him by the shoulders, while Romeo and I took his legs, and together we laid him as carefully as we could into the canoe, where he rocked on the water gently.

Black Fox crossed his arms. Our presence had disturbed something. Rustling sounds of attentive curiosity came from the hardwoods, and from the undergrowth. Then came the slosh of water and the cry of a screech owl.

Before he pushed the canoe further into the water, Black Fox took a handkerchief from his pocket. He undid the container top and placed it into the opening. He put the can by Harper's feet, lit the handkerchief, and stood back. There was a woosh and very quickly the canoe lit up, flames enveloping the man and boat in rolling waves.

Black Fox used his foot to push the canoe further into the water. The heat from the flames made my eyes water. It was as much of a burial ceremony as any, I guess. The wind hustled, and I became, I believe, in that moment, more attuned to the sound of water sluicing about the canoe and all about us in a kind of reverential movement, as if the elements themselves had conspired to transport Harper to another world.

And the fire – the fire was fierce and illuminated the misted waters about us in a pageant of autumnal burnishment; think orange, and red, and molten gold. Think damnation. And of course, the black smoke, which I imagined covering the body in a shroud of sorts. The fire gained in strength until it burned and roared and shone into the half-light like a beacon. Even the murk beneath the water's surface was irradiated with its luminosity. Wake up alligator. Receive ye snakes the body of our brother Harper. Afuckingmen.

The canoe floated in the water, almost serenely, a gentle current carrying it downstream. Then gradually it disappeared into a tunnel of mangrove and cypress which seemed to close about the deceased man and his vessel, and extinguish the light from the fire almost completely.

We looked at one another. There was nothing left to do.

'We are made from Mother Earth, we go back to Mother Earth,' Black Fox said.

We travelled back to the rez in silence. We were all worn out, not so much with the physical effort, but with the emotion of it all. It was draining. I felt spent, looked out at the landscape as we sped by, a haze and dazzle of sunshine. The sky was its familiar blue, and the clouds tumbled above us, oblivious to what we had done.

When we stopped by his house, Black Fox said, 'I guess it's time to say goodbye.'

'Logan,' I said.

'Let us deal with him.'

He got out, turned to go, but before he did, he said, 'you did the right thing,' though it felt to me that we had done nothing like it.

The next day was lost to me, but that night Blanchard was at his desk. The light was on, and I could see him bent over his paperwork. He must have heard the truck, but he didn't look up. Everything was still. There were no men walking the grounds. No one in the hammock on the barracks' deck. There wasn't any wind, hardly a sound to be heard. The echo of a siren in the distance, the steady hum of insects in the darkness.

I felt like I could take off, once and for all, leave this all behind. Then the feeling came over me again, as if this had all already happened. It stopped me in my tracks. My logic — accept what was going to happen because it had already happened. After what had taken place with Meribel, I felt a connection to Blanchard, a bond, as if we were linked now, like brothers.

I walked around the house. The dry grass broke beneath my feet. I waited. My breathing became slower. I found a spot beneath the jacaranda and sat. Above me the stars were brightening.

I sat there for the longest time. I thought about Harper, and Lola, and the mess we were all in. I felt trapped – like a character in a play. How to step out of it and break the spell? Stage left. Bright exit.

I watched an anger in me rise and fall. I waited for it to rise again, but by that time the stars had begun to fade, and it still wasn't clear to me what I was going to do.

I stayed for the rest of the night, thinking, not thinking.

The next morning I went back to work; and it wasn't until that afternoon that Blanchard asked to see me. We walked through the fields and he examined the clean-up.

'It's nearly back to normal,' he said.

I wondered was he joking. I wondered was he out of his mind. The place was a long way from back to normal. I was sure he would want to talk about Harper, and the ghost orchid, but he didn't. He looked exhausted. His eyes were sunken into his head, his cheeks hollow.

'Meribel,' he said, and I thought, *here it comes. This is the end.*

He cleared his throat in his formal way.

'I never thanked you for bringing her out,' he said. 'She had a swell time.'

He watched me closely. Swell, I thought. *Swell?*

'I'm glad,' I said.

'The play?'

'Yes?'

'How was it?'

'Dark.'

'It wouldn't have been my cup of tea.'

'She said you chose it.'

Blanchard paused, looked at me carefully. 'She did,' he said.

'Well, not my cup of tea either,' I said. 'Normally.'

'You hid it well. Meribel said you were wonderful company. I can't thank you enough.'

I mustered the gall to say, 'No need,' and wondered how much she had told him, and how much of this interview was a test. Blanchard's smile was hard to read, his expression a mask. Who knew what current of emotion ran beneath it, or what he was thinking or feeling? I hated that she was with him still, that he had that hold over her, but I was also used to this kind of agony.

We stopped by the tamarind.

'It was Logan,' I said.

'What now?'

'Who killed Harper.'

'Romeo told you that?'

'Yes.'

There was a deep black scar in the tree's trunk where it had been hit by lightning. Tamarind seeds lay scattered about its remains. Blanchard glanced at the tree one last time and turned. He didn't even offer the mildest directive to clear the debris.

'We need to …' I offered.

'We can't,' Blanchard said. 'And we won't. Not if we want the Garden to survive.'

'The Beast …'

'No more talk of them,' he said.

I knew the next number of weeks would involve turning the tamarind into firewood and filling the crater it left behind with soil. And I knew the pain of Harper's death would gnaw away at me until it was unbearable. But Blanchard said nothing more. He simply whistled as he made his way back to the house. He didn't even ask what we'd done with the body.

It was then the thought returned – or the seed of a thought. There had always been the possibility of violence within me. But now I felt something different. A shift had happened – as if a shadow-self had stepped further into the place where I was supposed to be, as if it had taken a little more control, and a little more of *me*. And what it said, and what it wanted was something bloody and calamitous, something murderous even.

The next day, I tried to lose myself in work. I raked leaves, fixed the legs on two trestle tables, and looked to some of the fencing on the perimeter which needed attention. It was good to be outside watching the clouds above me scud by, the sky's blue firing into a purple haze where a storm was whipping up somewhere far off in the distance. Who knew what direction it would take?

Romeo was busy in the lab, keeping the ghost alive, tending to it. I envied him a little, his know-how, his expertise, how the lab was his domain now, almost exclusively.

But what of it, I said to myself. I thought about Meribel then, imagined us together again, her hands, and lips, her neck. I was lost in that reverie when Romeo came to me.

'Come on,' he said. 'Time to take a break.'

I looked up at him.

'Sure,' I said.

We walked to the truck.

'This place will drive you crazy,' he said.

'But you have what we wanted.'

'Yes,' he said, 'and it's a fine species.'

'It'll survive?'

'With the right care.'

We got into the truck and made our way onto the highway. Cars were weaving their way in and out of traffic; the windows were rolled down. I loved that feeling of going somewhere. I looked up to see a plane's vapour trail disappear into nothingness.

'Where're we going?' I asked.

'The hospital.'

'Oh yeah, something the matter,' I said, assuming it was his arm.

His sling was gone, but the wound still needed to be re-bandaged. In fact, the current bandage was caked in dried blood and dirt. It needed to be changed, I thought, and his wounds needed some attention too, no doubt. But he never answered my question. Instead, he said, 'You and Meribel?'

'What now?'

'You heard me.'

'What of us?'

'What is there to tell?'

'Nothing.'

'Playing with fire, Swallow,' he said. 'Con fuego.'

As we turned into the driveway of where it was he wanted to go, I saw a large ivy-clad building. It looked more like a country home than a hospital. The gardens were well kept. The greenery on site neat and tidy. I saw two black gardeners working. Some patients walked the grounds on their own. Others looked to be chaperoned.

'We're here to see a friend,' Romeo said to my enquiring look.

'A friend?'

'Catfish.'

I shook my head.

Romeo said, 'If I'd told you, you wouldn't have come.'

'What's wrong with him?'

'He shot himself at boot camp.'

'He shot himself?'

We checked in at reception, where a woman asked us to write our names in the visitors' book and to say where we were from. I signed, then Romeo took his bandaged arm and slid it across the page. He wrote his name, then *The Garden*, and underlined it with a flourish. The receptionist inspected the book and looked at us curiously before directing us to the ward.

The smell was fusty, and there was a certain languor about the place, as if everyone was medicated, even the staff. Before we took the stairwell, we stopped at a small shop. Romeo bought a bag of grapes.

'He shot himself?' I said.

'Not on purpose. At least I don't think so.'

When we found the ward, Catfish's bed was empty.

'Where is Hugo?' Romeo asked the male nurse on duty. So that was his name.

'It's recreation time.'

'Recreation?'

'He's probably walking the grounds.'

Romeo dropped the bag of grapes on the bed, and we went back down. A nurse outside pointed to the maze. We sat on a bench and waited.

'A curious thing, don't you think?' I said to Romeo.

'Why is that?'

'A labyrinth in an institution of this kind? It could cause even greater confusion.'

Romeo shrugged.

When he emerged from the maze, Catfish was talking to himself. He was on crutches and unaccompanied. Romeo waved, and Catfish stopped and waved back, but otherwise he didn't betray any other sign of recognition.

'Mira,' he said as we approached.

Romeo asked what had happened, and Catfish turned his head. We went back to his ward, and Catfish took the bag of grapes from his bed and lay down. His bedside locker was covered with bars of candy and cans of Coke. He opened the bag of grapes then and ate them one by one.

'Sorry,' he said when he'd finished them. 'I didn't know how hungry I was …'

Romeo waved his hand, and Catfish held a finger to his lips, 'Shh,' he said. 'They could be listening.' He turned the knobs on the bedposts as if they were radio transmitters or something. 'The whole place is wired,' he said.

'This is a psych ward,' I whispered to Romeo, but he pretended not to hear me. A nurse came and said that visiting hours were over.

I looked carefully at Catfish. His leg was bandaged, his eyes appeared to be bulging in his head.

'You didn't make it through boot camp,' Romeo said. 'Not even boot camp.'

'I got shot,' Catfish said matter-of-factly.

'Who shot you?' I asked.

Catfish shrugged. 'Don't know.'

'Looks sore,' I said, and wondered was there a wound at all.

Catfish yawned. 'There's a bed here for you, if you want.'

Romeo got up to go to the john.

'His papa is worried about him,' Catfish said drowsily. I noticed the gold from his teeth was gone.

'I thought his old man was dead?' I said.

'Dead? No.'

'That's what he told me.'

'No, his papa is my uncle …'

'You guys are cousins?'

'Yeah, and I talked with him, and he wants to know how his mijo is.'

'What did you tell him?'

'He is a success, no?'

'And his mother?'

'She also worries about him.'

I put more questions to him about the farm he had grown up on. None of it matched what Romeo had said, bar the fact that they were involved in some turf war and Catfish had tried to escape it by joining the military.

Romeo returned, and we said farewell.

We didn't talk on the way back to the Garden, but later, on the deck, I lit a cigarette and asked Romeo what had really happened to Catfish.

'Like he said, a firearm was discharged.'

I thought this was believable, though there was a question mark as to whether the gunshot was self-inflicted, or whether Catfish had actually been shot at all.

I passed the cigarette to Romeo. 'Will he go back?' I asked.

Romeo turned to look at me, his face clouded in smoke, his eyes widening. 'I don't think he wants to,' he said.

Later, after we'd gotten back from the hospital, I got into the truck and drove to Lola's. I didn't expect her to be there, but she answered.

'There he is,' she said when she opened the door. She had been drinking. Everything looked a little lopsided about her – her face, her smile, the apartment behind her. Her coordination was not good. She swayed from side to side and tried to give me the bottle in her hand. I took it.

I said, 'Where were you?' and wondered about her neighbours and the apartment reception denying her tenancy, let alone her existence. The smell of weed was strong. The place in its usual disarray, the floor covered in clothes, magazines and sandals.

She responded by saying, 'Fuck you. What are you, my keeper?'

At first, I tried not to step on anything, but it was impossible. The air conditioner stuttered, then stopped. Lola kicked it and cursed. I asked her again where she'd been. She said quietly, 'Nowhere.'

I told her about the Chinese woman in the apartment office who said, 'no Lola.'

She thought this was hilarious. I asked her if she knew Deckards had burned down. She said, 'Sure.' I asked did she know what had happened. She said, 'Nope.'

I went to get a beer from the fridge, but the fridge was gone.

I said, 'So?'

'Here,' she said, handing me a warm beer from behind the sofa.

'What happened to the fridge?'

'Refrigerator?'

'Yeah.'

'Desiree took it.'

'Desiree?'

'Crack bitch neighbour,' she said.

'Okay. Why did she do that?'

'How the fuck do I know? Maybe she needed a *refrigerator.*'

'Maybe she did.'

'Saw her man take a shit on the balcony.'

'On the balcony?'

'In a bucket.'

'Time to move?'

'Fuck you.'

We sat and drank and smoked. We listened to Dave Matthews. At some point in the night, a car skidded in front of the complex and fired shots. We didn't dive, take cover or pray. We didn't do anything. Instead, we watched as a golden hand reached out into the dark.

Lola looked at me. 'Fuck,' she said.

In the shots' wake, there was an eerie silence. There were no sirens, no cars, and no screeching brakes. There was rainfall and darkness. That was all. We drank and smoked. We wondered who the shooters were, what they were after.

'Another attempt on my life,' I said.

'You think they came for you? You're crazy.'

'Maybe it's the orchids.' I pointed to the supermarket-variety orchid on her kitchen table.

'Huh?'

'I think there's something about them that makes people crazy.'

'Oh yeah?'

'When I look at a flower like the orchid, I think of Romeo and Miguel. I think of Blanchard and the stinking barracks I sleep in. I think of how a seed was blown from some place far off like Cuba or farther still, or how someone might have smuggled it, and what their journey was like. I think about the village they travelled from, their mother and father and all their struggles, and I think about when a flower like the orchid finds its way to a place it can grow, it needs air, and light, and water. How it needs to be looked after.'

I said the ghost orchid puts people under a spell. They want it but cannot have it. It's like the goblet in that poem. It puts you under a spell, so the wrong ones can't find it. So they can't get saved.

'Get saved?' she said.

'It's about salvation, I guess.'

And she said something about Jesus. And I said, 'No, Jesus doesn't have to be the one to save you. You can save yourself.'

'You really believe that?'

'The ghost orchid is part of that secret. It looks like a ghost. And what is a ghost? It's the presence of an absence. It's the embodiment of memory. It's a suitcase emptied of disappointment, out of which a different self can unfold itself one day after another. It's your mother talking to you from the grave. It's her fingers reaching out to you.'

She kissed me. We smoked and drank. We made love. Afterward, she took a shower and I lay listening to the air conditioner strain and shake. When she came out of the bathroom, water dripped from her hair onto her back, and she lay down next to me, and we made love once again before falling asleep. The next morning, she was up before me. I woke to hear the coffee machine dripping.

'I heard Romeo say something like that,' she said to me when I came into the kitchen. She was smoking a joint.

'Like what?'

'Like what you said last night.'

I didn't know what she was talking about. I was trying to remember, when I saw an item of clothing by the armchair I recognised. It was a maroon hoodie.

'What's that?' I said.

'Nothing.'

I stood up.

Lola said, 'Don't worry about it.' This was a favourite expression of hers. She used it every time she wanted to lock down the conversation. But the item of clothing – I couldn't let it go. I'd been blind-sided.

'Romeo's been here?'

'It's not important.'

I took the roach from her hand and pulled. 'You might have told me.'

Lola said, 'Why did you come over?'

My brain was a fog. 'To see you.'

'To fuck me.'

'Not if you've been with Romeo.'

She smirked. 'You can talk?'

'What did you say?'

I was standing now. She was too. I was in her face – the two of us breathing hard.

'You heard me.'

She took a step back. I took a step forward.

'Are you going to hit me now?'

I looked at her. Who was this woman? Who was she now?

'Jesus, I wish you would, you fucking pussy. Hit me.'

I raised my hand and made a fist, then dropped it and stepped back.

Lola started to laugh. Her laughter was shrill and insistent. And with the laughter came tears.

'You fucking asshole,' she said.

What was I doing here? Around me, everything looked cheap, and dirty. The smell of perfume, the beaded curtains, the unwashed sheets. The overflowing laundry basket, the clothes strewn about the floor. The naked orchid on the kitchen table. And Romeo's hoodie. It felt like I was only noticing these things for the first time, and with it the scratching sounds behind the walls, the scuttling cockroaches somewhere in the dark corners of the room. She went to the bathroom door and threw up in the toilet.

'Lola?'

She was on her knees. She turned and wiped the vomit from her mouth.

'Fuck you!' she said.

I looked once more at the shambles of the place, took Romeo's hoodie and left.

When I got back to the Garden, it was dark. I walked the grounds. I felt like a caged animal, cramped and confined. I couldn't shake Lola from my mind, her or her touch, or her betrayal. Once America had felt like a place to go in order to escape; now it felt like a prison to me. And Lola was one of its jailers.

I went to the shade-house and was considering the small batch of struggling epiphytes when Romeo approached. He suggested heading out.

'Not in the mood,' I said.

'Come on, muchacho. You need cheering up.'

He was at the truck, but it wouldn't start.

'Let's take the jeep.'

Miguel approached.

'He comes too,' Romeo said. I pointed to the back. Then Romeo said, 'I drive.'

'Fine,' I said. I threw him the keys and he handed Miguel an envelope.

'What's that?' I asked.

'Seedlings,' Miguel said.

'For who?'

'A guy asked,' Miguel answered. 'I said I'd give him a sample.'

'A guy?'

'Just someone.'

We took Krome, came to the interstate and made time. Romeo stopped at the Civic Centre.

'Why here?' I said.

'It's where he's meeting us.'

'I don't know, Romeo,' I said. 'I don't like this.'

'Don't worry about it,' he said.

I couldn't help feel a quiver of nausea at the words and the echo they made of what Lola had said to me. Miguel got out and walked up the steps to the Civic. A man approached him. He was tall, native, long-haired and in a black tracksuit. They talked. The man handed something to Miguel. Miguel handed the man the envelope. Then he made his way down the steps, faster and faster.

'What's going on?' I said to Romeo.

Miguel was running now. Behind him was another man, a larger man with long dark hair. He wore a sweatsuit and sneakers. There was a wild look in his eyes. Miguel swung the car door open. He jumped in.

'Drive!' he screamed.

The man was closing on us. Miguel had the wad of money in his hands. Then Romeo pulled away, but not fast enough. As we veered onto the highway, the man jumped onto the roof rack and started to kick the back windscreen in. Curses and prayers issued from Romeo. The windscreen shattered; the man swung at us with an outstretched arm. The jeep swerved.

'What are you doing?' I shouted.

Romeo was wild-eyed. 'Trying to shake the cocksucker,' he hollered.

The man fell to the tarmac and rolled. He stood up, wiped himself down, then held up a hand. Strange – it wasn't a wave or a salute, more a kind of mute acknowledgement. He stood on the motorway, cars driving around him, watching us career away into the distance. The wind rushed through the smashed back windscreen.

'What now?' I said.

Nothing from Romeo. No words. Just his blank and defiant concentration, and then after twenty miles, I said, 'What did you do?'

We pulled off the highway and drove down one minor road after another, until we came to a village with a repair shop. Romeo killed the engine and we got out to inspect the damage.

'What just happened?' I said. 'Who were those guys?'

'Miguel promised them ghost embryos.'

'No.'

'But that's not what he gave them.'

'Some peony seeds. Worthless,' Miguel said. He was grinning, but the colour had drained from his face.

'How did you know they would pay without checking?'

Romeo lit a cigarette, and sighed deeply, 'I didn't,' he said.

I looked at him. 'Who the fuck are you?'

We left Blanchard's jeep in to be repaired.

'That was a really dumb thing to do,' I said. 'You don't think trying to get the god-damn ghost was enough?'

Romeo said, 'I'm hungry.'

'Fuck,' I said, and we went to a place and got pizza.

'I was just helping a hombre out,' Romeo said when I looked at him at the table. We ate, wandered the streets, waiting for the car to be repaired, then found ourselves in a second-hand record shop. 'Hiding in plain sight,' I said. Romeo shrugged, flicked through the catalogue, and bought a single. I shook my head.

On the way back to the car shop we met a man standing on the street corner. He looked lost. He wore jeans and a denim jacket. No shirt. The jacket open. His fair, freckled skin was tinged and torn by sunburn. His bald head had heat scabs on it. His face was agitated. He moved awkwardly in leather cowboy boots. He wore no socks, and he was speaking, trying to tell us something. In his hand was a piece of paper.

'What you got, brother?' Romeo asked him.

He said something. I wasn't quite sure what the words he spoke were.

'Come again, brother?' Romeo said. The man muttered, swaying back and forth. Romeo opened his eyes wide and looked at me. 'He wouldn't be one of your own brethren?' he said imitating the man's rural voice.

I shrugged, and Miguel just stood and watched.

Romeo was having fun, 'Is he speaking the old tongue?'

'I don't think so,' I said.

The man held the piece of paper up to us. I looked at it curiously. Was it a map? He turned it one way, and another. Then Romeo snatched it from his hands and studied it. He started to laugh. He laughed so hard, he held his sides.

'Give it here,' I said.

The man swayed and shivered. The skin was peeling from the bridge of his nose. His hands shook. I can't be sure he saw what we saw when he looked across the highway and into the distance. His bleary eyes blinked, as if he couldn't focus, or as if he couldn't believe the things he saw.

I looked at the cyphers on the page. Not even the key to the arcane symbols of some ancient cult could have made these mad scribbles more intelligible. Somewhere there was the echo of an alphabet, but the drift of unreason had upended each letter. The sentences marched off their lines and dived about the page of print.

It was, we discerned, a message of some kind. That was clear. But the man's tongue was tied. By drink. By sleeplessness. By loss of reason. The sun and the sauce had him licked. He struggled. He wasn't an old man, either. But age had caught up and beaten him down.

'Shit,' Romeo said. 'I don't know what we can do for you bro. I mean you're not making any sense for a start.'

Miguel placed his hands in the man's pockets.

'What are you doing?' I asked.

'Seeing if the man is solvent.'

'Give him a few bucks,' I said, when Miguel had turned his pockets out.

'He needs the drunk tank,' he said.

'Yes, that or a hospital.'

'He'll die in this sun,' Romeo said. 'Take this,' he added, handing the man a twenty-dollar bill. 'Go get yourself watered.' He pointed to a bar across the street. The man squinted, but he didn't move. After a time, we left him mumbling and wavering in the setting sun.

Something upset me about the encounter. Was it because he reminded me of my father? Maybe. I sometimes wondered if the man ever made it where he needed to get to, or was he gone like the rest? Either way, we picked up the jeep, paid for it and drove.

'One more stop,' Romeo said.

'Oh Christ,' I said. 'This can't be happening.'

It was the hospital.

'Un momento.'

Romeo got out and walked towards reception.

'Fuck man,' I said to Miguel. I was looking at his reflection in the rear-view. 'What the fuck were you thinking?'

He shrugged. A man older than me, he looked like a schoolboy who was in trouble again. It was a role, I guess, he had never grown out of.

'If you needed money, you could have asked me.'

He pursed his lips. 'Hmmm,' he said, and then, 'I've asked too many times.'

Then I saw them coming towards me.

'You know,' I said to no one in particular, 'sometimes I think I'm living in someone else's fucking nightmare.'

There was Romeo, with Catfish in tow.

When we got back to the Garden, Romeo remained unnerved. He climbed into the hammock and closed his eyes. He placed his hands on his chest. I sat in the rocking chair. Miguel and Catfish sat on the steps drinking beer. Then Romeo got up and put the record on an old turntable Blanchard had donated to the barracks.

'Do you know who those guys were?' Miguel asked.

'What guys?'

'The guys we sold the seeds to …'

'Seminole?'

'Miccosukee.'

My head dropped. A rival tribe to the Seminole. They had fought recently over water rights. We did not need to be the instigators of further tensions between the tribes.

'That just made things a whole lot worse.'

'Sí,' he said.

The music from the record Romeo had bought played out from the barracks onto the deck. *We're on the road to nowhere.* Each time it came to the end, Romeo got back up and replayed it. I was too wired to go to my bunk and sleep. I just rocked back and forth as we spun in our orbit. Romeo came and sat on the stoop.

'If Logan hears about this, he's going to go fucking loco,' I said.

'No shit.'

'Then why the fuck did you fix it?'

'I didn't,' Romeo said looking at Miguel.

'Oh please,' I said. 'You've got to be shitting me.'

'Not me.'

He explained how Miguel had come to him, and pleaded with him as one Latino brother to another, that it would be no big deal, a small piece of trading with zero risk, and a big reward for him. That it would help him pay off a drug debt to Logan. I told him he was a fool for falling for any of Miguel's shit. He said he didn't want to see a brother in trouble, and didn't know about the Miccosukee; that was all Miguel's doing. Logan would hear, the world we lived in was small, and he wouldn't like it. That much was obvious, but what he would do about it was another thing. Who knew the heart and appetite for revenge a man like that might have?

Later, I walked the tunnels. Up and down. Back and forth. I could smell the sweet odour of fertiliser, and the whiff of chemicals, could hear the last of the orchids breathing in the dusky air and beat collectively like some kind of heart in the centre of the Garden – keeping us all alive somehow. And in the lab, the mother of them all, the ghost.

I went to chop wood. After a time, I heard something, a disturbance. A ripple of voices, an annoyance. Some of the men were giving out. It was about Romeo and his record. Of course it was. 'Turn it off,' they said. 'We need to sleep.'

Eventually, he got up and turned it off. The silence was abrupt. For a time that was enough, but it wasn't long until the stillness was broken. It was Romeo again. The sound of him stripping off and then the sight of him walking through the barracks naked. His clothes lay in a heap. His footfall sounded into the grounds. He must have got some shit from Miguel; he was off his head, and returning to nature. I saw him approach the jacaranda and put his arms around it. He started to talk to it. I thought about intercepting, getting the man to bed, but decided against it. Let him ride it out, I thought.

I went back to my bunk, and this time, I locked the barracks' door. As I drifted off to sleep, I heard the sound of Romeo's words in Spanish. It sounded to me like he was seducing the tree in his embrace.

My own dreams were of gnarled and tangled roots spreading under and over the Garden, transporting me back across a body of water to Ireland. I imagined my brother was calling my name. He was reaching out to me, and his arms were wrapped by roots which swirled about his body until they covered his face, and it was not just my name that he spoke.

I had set an alarm to wake early and left my bunk before anyone else had stirred. I loved the early morning. It was untainted, untouched by human interference. It was a time and place where a body could empty itself of the noisy night-time dreams and compose itself for the day to come. I looked to the sky, a pure blue, a configuration of faint cloud moving slowly above me. I looked at the ghostly formations as if they held a message in their shifting shapes, but there was nothing I could decipher. The others stirred and got to work. Then, I was told Blanchard wanted to see me. He was in his office in the main house.

'What are we going to do about Romeo?' he asked without preamble.

'What do you mean?'

'He's gone rogue.'

'Rogue?'

'I'm worried he's taking matters into his own hands.' Blanchard stubbed out the cigar he'd been smoking. 'What can you tell me?'

'There's nothing to report,' I lied.

He regarded me suspiciously. 'But you two, you go out together.'

'Sometimes.'

He pushed back his chair and stood. 'Let's discuss this off site,' he suggested. 'In more detail.' He asked me to drive to a bar. 'Sure,' I said, but I was a little confused. He had gone out of his way to hire Romeo, even while letting the others go; had given him access to the lab to breed what Romeo had christened 'the ghost moon'. And now here he was asking me what we were going to do about Romeo, saying he had gone rogue. Maybe he'd heard something.

I parked the jeep and we went into a bar called the Harp. I'd tried to avoid the Irish scene abroad, but Blanchard liked this watering hole. He liked the three republican sisters from Achill who owned it. He liked the lore and the romance of rebellion.

We ordered and then Blanchard said, 'The thing is I don't know if Romeo can be trusted.'

'He works hard,' I said.

Blanchard ordered whiskey chasers before we had finished our beers. Tammy Wynette was on the jukebox.

'But can he be trusted?' he repeated.

'I don't see why not?'

'What if he were to sell the ghost moon or its seedlings to someone else?'

'I thought that was the plan.'

'I have buyers lined up. Buyers who will pay a lot, but only if it remains exclusive. I don't want him selling dime-store prices to a back-alley black market.'

Blanchard turned to appraise me. This interrogation was tiresome. It felt like he was completely serious, but also having fun. A dour kind of fun, mirthless, and at my expense. He removed his red bandana and wiped his brow. He knew something, but wasn't letting on.

A man walked into the bar. He saw the two of us and walked straight out. Blanchard smiled at me and raised his glass.

'It's all fucked up,' he said.

'Maybe it's time to call it a day.'

'What do you mean, Swallow?'

'Harper's death. It's got out of hand.'

'But we're in too deep now. It would be more tedious to wade back than it would to keep on.'

'Keep on?'

'Finish the job.'

'But a man's been killed.'

'It wasn't our doing,' he said.

'But the blood is on our hands.'

'Blood will have blood.'

I'd never really seen Blanchard like this. He wasn't himself. His composure was gone, and he was drunk too quickly.

'We need to speak with Black Fox,' he said.

'You think?'

'Logan could pose further problems.' He looked into his glass, raised it to his lips, and swallowed hard. 'Did I ever tell you that my father killed himself?'

I shook my head. I couldn't tell if he was being serious.

'A Midwestern businessman, a success, a man who blew his brains out with a Smith & Wesson. I found him.'

His eyes narrowed on me.

'Pretty inconsiderate, don't you think?' he said. 'Even if he did have the good manners to leave a note. My mother never recovered. She kind of shrunk, every day a little more, until she disappeared quite literally from this earth.'

He was drinking like it was his last night on earth, as if he had no other choice than to down one beverage after another.

I went to say something, but he interrupted. 'We need to speak with Black Fox. I worry he's lost control of that nephew of his.'

'Didn't we buy the ghost, fair and square?'

Between gritted teeth he said, 'I made a promissory note for someone to guide us to the ghost orchid. We didn't buy the fucking thing. Only its whereabouts. We both know that we bought that knowledge on a promise. We bought that information on credit. That is all. They do not supply receipts for that kind of information, Swallow.'

He downed his whiskey, turned to me, and licked his lips.

'And about Harper, you better not tell anyone where you buried that old dog. Not even me.'

His head dropped to the bar top. Before I'd had a chance to ask if he was alright, he raised his head briefly, and said, 'Dismissed.'

I threw the keys of the jeep onto the bar and walked out to the highway to hail a cab.

I rang Black Fox and arranged to meet him at the rez that night. When I got there, he was sitting on a swing in a rundown playground on the outskirts. He was watching some kids come down the slide and play in the sandpit. Maybe they were his kids. He swung back and forth and watched the children with a gentle smile. When I came closer to the perimeter of the playground, he stopped swinging. He pulled on the lapels of his suit, took a handkerchief from his pocket and wiped something from his cowboy boots.

'Tough night?' he said.

I guess I looked like I'd been through the wringer.

'Something like that,' I said.

'Dark times,' he said. 'No one is safe.'

'Yeah.'

He smiled. 'You keep coming back. Now why is that?' he asked.

'I didn't cause this.'

'This …?'

'Why Harper?'

'Why any man?' he said, and lifted a bottle of beer to his lips.

I kicked at the dirt. 'We have to stop this. There's been too much …'

He stood from the swing and tossed the bottle to the ground before him. 'Too much what? Bloodshed.'

Suds from the bottle trickled onto the soil.

'Yes.'

He called out to the kids and told them to go home. They scattered from the playground. Then he lit a cigarette.

'A white man has come to tell me there has been too much bloodshed?' He let out a low and interminable laugh.

'Please,' I said.

'You've brought a white flag?' he said, smoke escaping from his mouth.

The sky was darkening. A deep rumble shook the calm.

'Logan gave Harper a beating. He went too far. I regret it. You know that,' he said.

'I want to avoid anything else from happening.'

'Like what?'

'Any other retaliations.'

'Why would there be?'

'Miguel …'

'The man who sold the ghost embryos to the Miccosukee.'

'So you do know?'

'We don't always see eye to eye with the Miccosukee. You read the news. Even a white man knows that.'

'So?'

'I've tried to control …' He cleared his throat and corrected himself, 'I've tried to manage my nephew. It's not easy. Our youth are disadvantaged, troubled. Add to that narcotics.'

'But …'

'But nothing. Blood is thicker – always. And that boy – he has the blood of his forefathers running thick through his veins. He's a warrior.'

'Logan?'

'You know, some of us call him Raised by Wolves.'

'And was he?'

'What do you think?'

'I heard his father's white.'

'What of it?'

'People say it turned him.'

Black Fox stepped towards me. I wasn't quite sure what he planned to do. His hand went to his pocket, but then a kid ran back into the playground and handed Black Fox a bottle of beer. He put his arm around the boy.

'His father is dead a long time.'

I breathed out the cool night air.

'Can you give me any assurances?' I asked.

He let out a world-weary sigh. 'I've done my best. But I can't make any promises as to what Logan will or will not do. Besides, I believe his issue with Miguel is not just about the seeds.'

In the shadows of the night his eyes looked to be filled with sadness.

'I'm getting old,' he said, straightening his back. 'Too old for battle.'

He began to walk away, his arm around the boy's shoulder. I got the sense that he was beaten down by the troubles his nephew had given him.

I called after them, 'Where is Logan anyway?'

Without turning, he said, 'I cannot tell you what I do not know.'

A thunderstorm struck again the next day. For part of the morning, the men remained in the barracks. But Catfish had his bags packed.

'I'll drop him to the airport,' Romeo said.

'Where is he going?'

'As far from trouble as he can get.' Romeo laughed.

'Good luck,' I said, and shook Catfish's hand.

He thanked me, and I said, 'de nada.'

I couldn't help think that it didn't matter where he went, that trouble would follow. He limped away, and looked behind, something inscrutable in his expression. Above us, the sky was a brilliant swirling mass of purple lights. The downpour was sudden and ended abruptly. What a strange presence Catfish had been, one of those who comes and goes, who drifts in and out of others' lives like a seed on the wind, powerless, it seemed, in their own way to take root.

When Romeo got back, we did the rounds and made sure everything was secure, locked down. I thought about him with Lola. Part of me didn't want to share her with him, hypocritical though this may have been. I didn't want to be a part of any shabby love triangle, but I also knew my affections now lay elsewhere. And anyway, I didn't know what to say about it. What I did do was put his hoodie on, and when I did so, he looked at me askance. I waited for him to say something, but he didn't, not then, and we carried on our rounds.

'A word to the wise,' he said in Spanish.

'What's that?'

'Blanchard.'

'Yes?'

'He's been asking about you.'

'About me?'

Romeo nodded earnestly. 'He's wondering ...'

'Wondering what?'

'If anything is going on.'

I didn't know whether to believe Romeo. I didn't know whether he was saying this because he had an inkling that Blanchard was asking about him or whether this was simply Blanchard rattling my cage. I could've told him the very same story. 'Blanchard's been asking about you.' I could've told him that Blanchard must be trying to set us against each other, but I didn't.

After our rounds, I took the hoodie off in front of him and threw it in the dirt.

'Where did you get that?' he asked.

'Not from your bunk.'

'No?'

'Maybe you left it somewhere?'

'Maybe.'

'Where did you leave it?'

'Let's not play games.'

'Who's playing games?'

He looked at the hoodie in the dirt and shook his head. He said something under his breath I couldn't make out, then he walked away. I spat on the ground and cursed.

Later, I heard raised voices from the main house. This was not unusual. It was well known that Blanchard and Meribel argued. Sometimes loudly, sometimes not. Nobody said or did anything about it. It was an unwritten rule.

What few men remained were playing cards, or had left for the weekend to return to families spread throughout the state or farther afield – elsewhere – that country where we told ourselves that things were worse, where people were poorer, sicker, without the means. Tonight, it had been eerily quiet. Even Romeo wasn't prowling, but had headed out to drink or gamble, or maybe gone to Lola's. I was restless, and walked the grounds. When I heard the crash of kitchen crockery, I found myself closer to the house than I'd expected to be. I felt more protective of Meribel after what had happened between us. Part of me had wanted to flee, and forget, but another part of me felt there was a connection between us now. I didn't want to see her hurt.

I made my way to the house, careful at first not to be seen, and looked in through a window. It was a wild affair – Meribel was walking from room to room, calling out, shouting and crying. She knocked something from a coffee table and it crashed to the ground. Blanchard followed her from one room to the next. His voice was bass, a low rumble. I heard her say that she'd had enough, that she was sick of hearing about the ghost, that it was destroying her, destroying them.

Then I heard him spit the words, 'You fucking bitch.' I heard a thump and slap. I ran to the door. I hesitated. I waited. I heard it again. The words. The blow. I kicked the door open. He was straddling her, a savage look in his eye, and he was punching her. She looked dazed. Then her head turned to the side – she took me in, but said nothing – and still Blanchard lay atop of her, panting and sweating like a wild animal.

I pulled him off her and struck him. He snivelled and hid his face behind his arm. 'Stop,' he said. I struck him again. 'Stop it.' He slumped back down, defeated, and lay side by side with his wife. It looked almost post-coital, but for the mess of blood. Blanchard sat up and looked at her. She held her hand to the wound, touched and tasted the blood.

'What are you doing here?' Blanchard said to me.

'Her wound needs stitching,' I said. 'You'll have to take her to the hospital.'

He stood, brushed himself off. 'I can't do that,' he said. 'They'll arrest me.'

Meribel said, 'I don't want there to be a scar any bigger than it needs to be.'

'Swallow,' Blanchard said. 'You take her.'

He took off his bandana to stem the flow of blood. 'There now,' he said. 'Hold it firm.'

He gave me the keys to the jeep.

'Do this for me,' he said.

'I've been drinking.'

'It doesn't matter. Drop her off at Emergency. She can get a taxi back. You can too.'

I went to Meribel.

'Bring her before she starts to get any ideas,' Blanchard said.

Meribel accepted his suggestion, and before I knew it, I was starting the jeep and driving. At that moment helping Blanchard was the last thing I wanted to do, but I wasn't doing it for him. Meribel needed to go to the hospital. I was helping her.

'Please don't tell anyone,' she said.

I said I wouldn't. I struck the steering wheel with my first. 'God damn,' I said. Then as I drove, she said, 'Can we not go to the hospital, please?'

'Where then?' I said, but she didn't answer, and I didn't know where to go, or what to do. I drove through the city, my heart filling with hate, past the late-night eateries, the bars, and underpasses, past the corner boys, and night time wanderers, the 24-hour convenience stores, the 7-Elevens, past a man eating a burrito on the sidewalk, and another drinking a beer, past a torn flag of the union flapping in the wind.

'Where are we?' Meribel asked when we arrived.

'Lola's.'

'From the bar?'

'Maybe you can stay with her,' I said. Then I thought: Romeo. Maybe he was here.

She came with, her hand still pressing the bloodied bandana against the wound. I knocked on the door.

'What do you want?' Lola answered without seeing Meribel.

'I'm sorry about the other day, but something's happened.' I put my arm about Meribel.

Lola stood back. 'Bring her in.'

'I wasn't sure whether I should go straight to the hospital or not.'

'Let me see her.'

Lola sat Meribel down and brushed the matted hair from her face and eyes. She was gentle and caring. I'd never seen her like this. She took Meribel's hand in hers. There was no sign of Romeo.

'I'm sorry,' Meribel said. Lola told her not to be.

'Can I have a glass of water?'

'I think you need something stronger, darling.'

I went to see what there was. I found a half bottle of vodka and poured us all a drink. Lola said thanks and then to Meribel she asked, 'What happened, sweetheart?' Meribel could hardly answer. 'I'm tired,' she said, sipping her vodka and coughing.

Lola looked to me.

'It was Blanchard,' I said.

Then the bandana slipped from Meribel's hand, and Lola said 'Fuck' when she saw the wound.

'You can stay here, but I think you need the hospital.'

Meribel began to weep. 'Shit,' she said.

'What?'

'It hurts when I cry.'

Lola looked at me, and said, 'Men are such pigs.' Then to Meribel, 'If I were you, I'd kill that son of a bitch. I'll even do it for you.'

Meribel laid her head on the couch.

'I'm so sorry this has happened to you,' Lola said, stroking her cheek.

She took a cloth from the bathroom, came back and dabbed the cut. Meribel flinched.

'Okay,' Lola said, 'so the blood has been stemmed, but the wound still looks like it needs attention.'

'Attention?'

'Stitches, several would be my guess. Should I come with?'

'No,' I said. 'I'll take her. She just didn't want to go straight.'

'I get it, but take her now and hurry.'

Before we left, Lola gave Meribel a hug. She said, 'You're going to be okay.'

I drove fast, weaving through the traffic, blowing the horn when I needed to, speeding when I didn't. I parked quickly and led Meribel to ER. At reception, a woman took her name and asked for mine.

'Relationship?'

'Friends,' I said.

I waited with her. Four others sat in the waiting room. Ill-looking and down in the mouth. A mother with a child who had what sounded like whooping cough. Others walked in and out. The smell of the hospital brought me back to when I was a child, the antiseptic, the stitches, the broken bones.

'Coffee?'

Meribel shook her head. I got it anyway.

'Here,' I said. 'It might help.'

The bandana was drenched in blood. I threw it in the trash. The blood had stained her hands, and she looked at them desolately. The clock ticked loud and slow above us. After an hour we'd not seen a doctor or nurse, and the receptionist had gone. One of those waiting, a black man with a broken arm, stood and left through the exit doors without a word.

I got up and wandered through the corridors looking for someone to help us. The hospital seemed to be deserted. It was eerily quiet, but behind doors and curtains I heard the whispers of doctors, nurses and their patients. I looked at the time again, but the clock had stopped.

I found a nurse. She led Meribel to a dimly lit room. She lay her down and looked at her wound.

'Can he wait with me?' Meribel asked when the nurse went to leave.

'Yes,' she said. 'I'll get the doctor.'

Meribel asked me to lie on the bed with her. It was a single bed and I said there wasn't enough room. She pleaded and I did as she asked. We lay facing one another.

'I'm sorry,' I said, and she touched my face with her hand.

'Why sorry?'

'I should have stopped him.'

'No.'

'Maybe I could have. Maybe I should have even …'

'What?'

'Hurt him more.'

When the nurse came back, she came back with a cop. I sat up from the bed. I looked at Meribel, but her eyes were closed. The cop looked at me with contempt. Then the doctor arrived. She was a young woman. She cleaned the wound and began to stitch beneath the eye.

She went to look at me but stopped herself. When she'd finished, Meribel said, 'He didn't do it. He's a friend. He just brought me here.'

'I'll let you and the officer decide,' the doctor said, leaving.

The Beast approached me.

'If it wasn't you, who was it?'

'It wasn't him,' Meribel said from her bed.

The Beast looked at the bruises on my hands which had blossomed since I'd hit Blanchard. He led me away. Outside, he cuffed me and put me into the back of his cruiser.

'We're not going to the station,' he said. 'I'm arresting you on assault charges. You should be going to county, but I'm bringing you to jail.'

I didn't understand. It didn't matter. My mugshot was taken, my fingerprints too. I was placed in a holding cell. I sat down and a black man sat next to me. He asked me what I was in for. I tried to speak, but my voice was trapped inside me. He talked, but I couldn't understand what he said, or I didn't hear him. It was loud. There were about thirty or forty men in the cell. African-Americans, Hispanics, some whites. On one wall was a line of payphones. I was told I could make a phone call, but all the phones were in use.

I thought I would call Blanchard or Romeo. One man seemed to be finished using the phone. He was large, a couple hundred pounds, six foot four maybe. He held the phone in his hands and stretched the cord. Then he placed the receiver into the crotch of his tracksuit.

'Who needs to make a call now?' he shouted. 'Who needs to make a call?'

He laughed and shuddered and called out again. I closed my eyes. Time passed, I don't know how long. There were no windows, no way of knowing what time it was; the smell of the place was stale and foul. Later, an officer entered the cell. He called out my name, and I held up my hand. He approached me and asked me if I had a lawyer. I told him I hadn't. He said I could be assigned a lawyer by the State, and left. I sat for the rest of the night and thought about Meribel in her hospital bed, and the fist Blanchard had used against her. I did not sleep.

The next day, when the lawyer called my name, I was wavering between hallucination and nightmare. I went to him. He looked like a teenager. His face was young, his hair red, his eyes pale. He talked quickly, and softly, so that I found it difficult to hear him. He read the case-file summary. He said something like, 'If you don't plead guilty, you could be here for several months, if not the year, awaiting trial. If you plead guilty, with no priors, and your military record, I can get you out this week with a fine, and a slap on the wrist.'

Before I had a chance to say anything, he said, 'I'll come back tomorrow for your answer.'

More hours passed. I was approached by other men in the cell, was asked questions. I said nothing, didn't move. When food was handed out, I couldn't tell if it was breakfast or lunch. It was two slices of white bread with a slice of pale-yellow processed cheese. I looked at it, but I didn't eat. Instead, one of the other prisoners stood above me. I held out the sandwich, and he took it.

'Good boy,' he said. He turned to his friends and they laughed.

Later, I rang the main house. No one answered. I imagined Meribel had returned and was recuperating in bed, unable or unwilling to lift the receiver. Blanchard I imagined scowling at the instrument, or ripping it from the wall.

There was another phone in the lab, but its number was not something I had off by heart. I put the receiver down. I sat back against the grey wall and tried with all my energy to remember it, but could not.

The next day, I think it was the next day, the arraignment took place in a small room inside the jail. The judge appeared on a tiny TV screen hanging from the ceiling in the middle of the room. I could hardly hear or see him. The lawyer was in the room with me. Several statements or declarations or whatever you call them were said aloud. I couldn't make them out. I didn't understand.

There was an exchange about whether the hand which struck the victim – they maintained it was mine – was open or closed. If it was closed and made into a fist the sentence would mean twelve months in prison. If the hand was open, a slap instead of a punch, the sentence would be less. I stuttered my answers. The words were trapped in my throat. I wanted to tell them it wasn't me, but what the lawyer said came back to me.

'I couldn't give a fuck if you are guilty or not, if you hit her, or someone else did. I don't care. It doesn't matter. They caught you. You were caught. That's what I have. That's what I gotta deal with. So, are you going to play ball, or are you gonna rot away in prison?'

I believe these were his words, or a close approximation of them.

'And let me tell you one more thing before you answer. Military record or not, people like you were not made for the county jail. You hear me? You make me madder than a wet hen. They will chew you up and spit you out, and do it again and again until you can't take it. Until you end up in some psych ward in the boondocks. You hear?'

I had nothing to say to this. Not immediately. When he pressed, I said, 'But I didn't do it.'

'That's what they all say.'

'But I didn't.'

'And if we were to start an investigation, if we were to invite an investigation by the DPP, you will still sit and stew. Just let me get you out of here.'

I didn't know what to do or say.

His final caveat was, 'Be reasonable.'

To be reasonable was not to sleep. To be reasonable was to eat the non-food to keep up your strength, and fight when you had to fight, and to say to yourself, this too shall pass, and to pray again, and placate the black dog that came in the night, growling, and let it sit next to you. To be reasonable then was to admit guilt when it was not yours.

The lawyer's defence relied mainly on my good character. He called me an idiot for letting my papers expire, but cited 'Possible defences to the deportation of an undocumented alien'. There was also my lack of major priors. He called upon my military service. He mentioned too the medal I had been awarded. I hadn't told him, but he'd found out, which was useful, because the DPP were going to refer my case to immigration. He seemed confident that prosecutorial discretion could be used.

When they'd called my name, I'd been asleep. I was dreaming, dreaming that my brother and I were down by the river riding the tyre back and forth. Our friend Christian had come to play with us. He had fallen and hit his head. His eye bruised. Christian had asked us to walk him home. He was hurt and disorientated. He wanted his mother, whom he lived with. His father was gone. Jamie had put his arm around Christian and started to walk with him, and he'd mouthed some words of comfort before I said, 'Stop it'. I said that no, we wouldn't go with him, because we needed to get home.

Christian said nothing. Jamie appealed to me with his eyes, and I said we had to go, and we left him there – our friend – and we walked away, though there was nowhere we had to be, and nothing we had to do. It was less of a dream and more of a memory. Then I heard my voice being called, and a man shook me. He pulled me to my feet, and I was brought back into the waking nightmare once again.

My laces were returned to me, and with it my wallet, lighter and Harper's dog tags. Romeo was waiting in reception, shaking his head. He put his arm around me, and I nearly wept.

'Caballo,' he said as we walked to the truck, which in Spanish meant 'horse', and in Honduran Spanish is directed to someone who does something without considering the consequences. This he explained to me on the way back to the Garden. And then he said it again, 'Caballo.'

I couldn't get out of bed for days after. And then, everything was harder – work, the clean-up, the day-to-day grind. I wondered how Meribel was, how she was recovering, what she was thinking. As for Blanchard, I wanted to know what he had to say. I wanted to know what he was going to do. My anger at him had transformed itself into a simmering rage. I felt duped, used. I thought about what I could do to him to make him pay. I thought about feeding him to the coyotes.

When I asked Romeo about him, he said, 'There's nothing to say. He comes and goes. The buyers come and go. The sun and moon. The sun some more.' I knew what he meant. Everything had changed, and nothing had changed. He smiled at me. 'Welcome back to paradise,' he said.

'Fuck you,' I said, but I was smiling.

Still, I wanted Romeo to say something else. I wanted him to voice his concern, and outrage, but he had nothing to say on the matter. He thought I was a fool for taking the rap. That was all. He was all about the ghost, its resuscitation, its cultivation.

After work that night we went drinking at the local Mexican shebeen.

'Then again,' he said, 'if you hadn't taken the rap, what's the alternative?'

He cocked his thumb and shot at me. We drank. We drank some more. And with the alcohol the thought, the nagging possibility, slipped into my mind that this man before me, with all his bonhomie, might be the one to do it. That Blanchard may yet ask him to be the one to pull the trigger on me.

Back at the Garden, Meribel glided by one or other window frame, but she never emerged. She had not left him. I imagined the bruises healing, the scars taking shape. Sometimes the curtains to her bedroom remained closed for an entire day. Still, as I worked, I could sense her within, and I yearned to take away her pain.

Blanchard I saw walking to one of the dumpsters with a yellow duvet. It was stained with dried and blackened blood. He threw it in, wiped his hands and looked about him. He saw me standing on the barracks' deck. For a moment, we regarded one another. Then he spat and went back inside. Later that day, he came to me.

'Here,' he said. 'No hard feelings.'

I looked down to see what he'd put into my hands. It was a stash of fifty-dollar bills. President Grant staring back at me, the Civil War behind him, weeping alone at Lincoln's grave.

'Where did you get this?' I said.

'I've taken an advance on the ghost. You can pay your prison fine, and there's something extra besides.'

At first, I said nothing. There was the smell of burning leaves in the air. The sky was a dark purple. The hum of the earth seemed to flow through me. I handed the cash back to Blanchard. His hands trembled as I dug the notes into his palms.

'If you touch her again,' I said, 'I'll kill you.'

After that, Blanchard came and went even more so than he used to, doing deals, going to orchid shows, meeting with prospective buyers. His absence left ripples, small waves of disruption. He left notes or printed out messages and communiques before he set off. *Back Wednesday. Gone for some days. Will call with instructions.*

Nobody asked where he was, but the men did ask if he was around. They wanted to know when he'd return, but they didn't push the issue. They didn't want to disturb the relative peace which had descended upon the Garden. When I told the men Blanchard was out of town, they would smile secretly and go about their work. Business was the watchword.

Besides, I didn't seem to care anymore. Romeo was the only one who didn't accept the new atmosphere. He was still on guard, and I couldn't help but enjoy his discomfort. For hours on end, he would say nothing, whether he was working or not, as if he were mulling the ghost's survival and taking full responsibility for it. But mostly he worked at the lighting and temperature controls and toiled at his task.

'Not too hot, not too cold,' I heard him repeat time and again.

Water was important. He replaced the soil. There was something tortuous about his methodical care and expertise. It left me in the cold, but soon his torment became mine too. I may have indulged his agony and took some perverse pleasure in it, but, in many ways, we both suffered.

When Blanchard returned, often unannounced, his behaviour was erratic. He was a man on the edge. He started doing dawn patrols, circling the Garden with a shotgun, talking constantly of the threat from outside. Added to that was his stolid, silent presence; how he

watched everything and everyone with what looked like
unveiled suspicion; how he worried that someone was
going to take his new breed of ghost orchid or storm
the place in a dawn raid or whatnot. Then there was his
drunkenness, and the shots he fired after midnight at the
moon.

New security lights were installed. I guess, again, the
money must have come from a prospective buyer. He
got himself a new dog. A German Shepherd, which he
doted on. A puppy actually. He called it Gunter, after a
great uncle who'd fought in Korea. He spent more time
lavishing love and praise on the dog when saying goodbye
than he did his wife, petting it, lowering his head, trying
to look it in the eye and speak to it.

Gunter, whose coat was healthy, and whose pedigree
was true, was as indifferent to Blanchard's attentions as he
was to the rest of us. Before Blanchard left on any trips, he
gave me strict instructions on what to feed the dog, when
to walk and groom him. And in his absence, the dog and I
became friends. He even found his way into the barracks
at night to lie by the end of my bed. There was something
faintly soothing about his docility and canine snores.

One night, when Blanchard returned, and I was
patrolling the perimeter with Gunter, flashlight in hand,
he called the dog to him, but Gunter didn't come. Instead,
the dog whimpered and stayed by my side. Blanchard
approached. He looked dishevelled and worn out. Maybe
his international sales were not going as well as they could
have been. Who knows? He never discussed these things
in detail. He was disappointed too that the dog had not
gone to him, but he knelt nonetheless, and Gunter for
once accepted his attentions.

'What do you know?' he said, waving the light from
his face, but this time his words were directed not to me,
but to Gunter. Whatever there was left worth knowing,

Blanchard was content for it to be communicated by the relative silence of his pet. Of course, he may have been worried that Meribel would point the finger at him, but after I'd been arrested that would have meant a very complicated case. Still, fear will drive a man to pick up and leave at the oddest of hours. It will make him do and say the strangest things.

Then, before he left again for another trip, he came to me. 'Here,' he said, handing me a piece of paper. On it was the code to the safe in his house. He asked me to pay the men at the end of the month. 'On the Friday,' he said.

He stood back and kicked the dirt and smiled awkwardly. I know he resented the responsibility he was giving me, but he had no choice, I guess. At the same time, he made what he said about the code, and the money, sound like a great honour. Of course I would do it, I told him. There was no problem.

'Still,' he said, 'listen carefully.'

His instructions were strict. The cash was to be counted twice, notes ordered in descending denominations, face-up, and placed into a brown envelope.

He paused. 'Meribel will show you the rest.'

Then he touched my shoulder with his hand; it was an odd display of intimacy, or was it contrition? I sensed there was something about him that wanted to be away from the place, away from the site of his shame, though I imagine with the ghost in situ he was conflicted. He could always use a potential buyer as an excuse, or another orchid show. I don't know if he was expecting me to say something about the safe, the cash, or Meribel. Maybe he was expecting me to ask where he was going. But I didn't. I merely stepped aside.

'Well then,' he said. 'It's farewell for now.'

When the time came to pay the men, I called to the door. Meribel answered.

I asked her how she was, but of course it would have been a little forced for her to say, 'I'm fine.' And she didn't. And how could she be, in any case? I didn't know how or why she would have stayed with Blanchard after what had happened. She smiled, but said nothing.

I said, 'I'm here to …'

'I know why you're here,' she said.

Her tone was curt, harsh even. Unnecessarily so, I believed. I don't know why. I had only the most tender of thoughts for her. But everything that should have been said was not said. It felt too late somehow. I held up the piece of paper with the instructions for the safe, and she led me to Blanchard's office. Inside, there was the stale smell of cigar smoke. It felt like a long time since I'd walked into this house to shower, change and bring Meribel to the theatre. A long time since we'd been together.

'How are you?' I asked again.

'I'm … I don't know how I am. I'm sorry.'

'You don't need to be sorry.'

'And you …'

I shrugged.

'You took the rap?' she said.

'I shouldn't have, I guess.'

'I don't know. I'm confused. I don't know anything right now.'

We were standing within arm's length of one another. I could sense the energy of her body, its fear and desire.

'He's an animal,' I said.

She dropped her head. 'I can't just walk away …'

'Of course you can.'

'It's not that simple.'

'Isn't it?'

'The ghost—'

'Don't blame it.'

'If he hadn't become so obsessed with it … I tried to reason with him. I tried to stop him. I thought we could move on, rebuild elsewhere. But he wouldn't have it …'

I took a step towards her, and she came to me. She lay her head on my shoulder and we embraced.

'I won't cry for him,' she said.

I felt her hot tears on my neck. She stepped back and wiped them away.

She met my gaze. It felt like she was opening up to me, letting me in.

'Thank you, Swallow.'

The fan spun on its axis, unevenly, its blades wobbling above us.

'Stupid thing,' she said looking up to it.

I let her hand go, and said, 'I thought we might have …'

'What?'

'I don't know.'

'Run away together?'

'That was your idea.'

'I feel like we're trapped here,' she said.

'But we're not.'

She smiled, and shook her head, and stepped away from me.

Outside, the eternal sunshine. It felt like a curse at a time like this. It felt right then that it was for the earth and its flora and fauna, not for the likes of us, the mendacious creatures we were. We humans were better off skulking in shadows, licking our wounds, and talking in intimate whispers of betrayal and death. Not for the sunshine, not the light.

Meribel revealed the safe behind Blanchard's desk, hidden within the bookshelf.

'I didn't know he had the safe here,' I said. 'Not until he told me.'

'Why would you know?' she said.

'Is it secure?'

'It was before he told anyone. If it gets robbed, we know where to look,' she said.

'Sorry?'

'We'll be after you.' She was laughing now, her mood altered. Gaiety returning to her demeanour, the actress playing a role. 'Or he will.'

'Yes, right,' I said.

She held a finger to her mouth and smiled.

'I guess that was his logic. That he trusts you.'

'Or he has to …'

'Or he owes you.'

She ran her finger over a globe of the world, then spun it. Her movement seemed choreographed, as if she'd rehearsed the scene. Then, her hand went to the line of stitches beneath her eye.

'You think I wouldn't …' I said.

'What? Take the lot and run?' She laughed a little and went quiet.

'He didn't want you to pay the men?'

'Look at me, Swallow. Look at what he did to me. No, he did not want me to pay the men.'

I went to her, touched her face gently with my fingertips.

'What are we going to do?' I said.

She lowered her head. I thought we might have kissed then, but no, she stepped away, went to the safe and opened it.

'There you are,' she said.

On top of the stacks of notes lay a pistol. It was a Smith & Wesson, the one his father had shot himself with, I guessed. I knelt down to the safe, took the gun and weighed it in my hands. It was lighter than I'd expected. How could something so light take a human life?

I sat into the office chair and ran my finger over the desk's burnished green leather. Then I reached into the safe again and took the cash out. I counted it; and before I left, I took the gun.

The day stretched before me. Farther and farther, so that it seemed the night was out of reach. The hours stalled. The temperatures fell. The sprinklers doused the grasses in viscous beads of water. Above was the hum of a plane. No sight of it though, only the endless and eternal blue of the sky.

With it, the gentle sound of a breeze making its way through the long grasses about me. I was in the hammock trying not to think about what needed to be done when a man approached. He was swarthy and weather-beaten. Moustachioed, a hat in hand, his eyes restless and wary. He was looking for something, but reluctantly, as if he didn't want to be here at all. But it wasn't work he was looking for. It was Romeo.

'Romeo?' I said.

The man had heard he might be here.

'What about him?' I asked.

The man smiled. 'I thought you might know where he is,' he said politely. He took a white handkerchief from his pocket and wiped his brow.

I said I didn't know. He looked about him, surveying the Garden, without any great urgency. Then he asked about the orchids. He held his hat demurely in both hands and twirled it through his blackened fingers.

'What is he to you?' I asked.

'I wanted to know where he is. That is all.'

'I wish I knew,' I said.

'But you work with him?'

I swung back and forth on the hammock.

'Do you want me to give him a message?' I asked.

He hesitated.

'Is it about the orchids?'

'It's a delicate matter.'

Finally, I said, 'If you don't tell me, I can't help you.'

When I looked up again, the man was still there. I'd half expected him to be gone.

'Maybe I can talk to you?'

'About what?'

Miguel appeared and told me he needed help with the netting to one of the shade-houses. I sat up and shrugged at the old man. Finally, he held up his hand in farewell and left. I felt bad, as much for not finding out what he wanted as anything else. I got up and helped Miguel out. Romeo was there. The man need only have looked. He was on his hands and knees pulling at weeds. Who was he, I wondered? A buyer, or someone Romeo owed money to? Romeo said something about the fences, and something else about compost, and that he needed to get back to the ghost. His words washed away in the shimmer of the afternoon.

Then he looked up, and said to me, 'Lola.'

A line of black ants were making their way to the body of a dead toad.

'What about her?'

'I think she needs money,' he said.

'Lola always needs money.'

'I think she needs it soon.'

'Oh yeah?'

'Yeah, like now.'

'How do you figure that?' I said.

Romeo stood and wiped the dirt from his pant-legs.

'She's got problems,' he said with a squint.

I took a stick and poked at the toad. Its green body was covered with ants. It almost looked alive. Its new armour flickered in the sunshine. Gradually, the ants took the body of the toad apart. Soon shadow and blood would be all that was left of it, and that too would wither and fade in the sunshine's glare.

Then, as the ants dispersed, I realised who the man with the hat had been. He was one of the cooks in the kitchen at Deckards. He'd worked with Lola. I must have seen him once before. Maybe I'd drunk with him. He was here to tell me something, and I'd sent him away. It occurred to me he may not have needed to know where Romeo was – he could simply have been embarrassed.

'What problems?' I said to Romeo.

He waited for me to catch up, to get it. He sighed and shook his head.

'She's in trouble,' he said. And when I was about to ask him what kind of trouble, he simply nodded as if to say, 'Now you understand. Now you know what I'm trying to talk to you about.'

The man had come to ask for money on Lola's behalf, so that this scene we found ourselves in didn't have to happen, so Romeo didn't have to ask, or corner me into the dumb realisation of what the situation was and why she needed money. Her illness and disorientations made sense to me now. She was pregnant. Romeo, uncomfortable as he was, had avoided having to paint a picture. He'd shown discretion. I nearly choked on my own stupidity.

I looked down where the ants had been. They were gone, and so was the toad. I couldn't bear to ask Romeo whether the child was mine. Or what the situation was.

How had I not known? Right then, none of it seemed to matter. My mind was on fire. I dug into my pockets, and to my shame, I threw him the roll of hundreds that was there. The notes fluttered in the wind and fell to the ground. It's not what I'd meant to do, but it was too late.

'No,' he said quietly. 'It's not like that.'

He stood watching the cash blow in the dust before him. I was already walking away, but not before I saw him bend. The light dazzled my eyes, and it was like he was there and not there. And then, it was like I was watching myself bend and take the money back into my own hands.

Several days passed before I finally called her. It went straight to voicemail. Her recorded voice was nonchalant, and asked me to leave a message, asked anyone to leave a message. I didn't. I just hung up. What I'd done in the intervening time, I can't remember. The working hours had been a balm to me. The heat had penetrated my limbs, baking me into the submissive rhythms of mindless toil. That is what I'd wanted when I first came here. And that is what I got. Now, I felt the sun's intensity was on the wane. I felt the cold again, and with it the things I'd left behind wavered uncertainly in my mind. Work, booze, the ache of the past, the pull of desire – it made my memory unreliable.

I called again. This time the phone didn't even ring. The tone was dead. I was worried. I began to feel like I didn't belong. I went about my workday with a strange sense of dislocation. Not only from my surroundings, but from myself. I became detached, disembodied. It was as if I were watching myself from a distance or a height. I was a man with a spade in his hands, digging. I was a person apart, even from himself.

That night I went to her apartment. The streets were rain-soaked, but I watched the asphalt absorb it all, and steam away its devil's breath until the sudden downpour looked like it had never happened.

I stood in front of her door. I felt bereft. So much of our relationship had happened behind this panel, this gateway, and between her four walls. Our life together seemed bound to the apartment's existence. We had not been if it had not been, my mind seemed to suggest. The sadness weighed me down.

I raised my hand, but didn't knock. I was paralysed by uncertainty and fear. I didn't know what I would say, or what I wanted to say. Surely, we had reached the end of the road, whether we got to speak or not, whether she was with child; and whose child?

I turned to leave. As I made my way down the steps, my ears filled with noise, but within it, I heard her door open. I froze. Then the door closed behind her and she came down the stairwell and the noise in my head came to a crescendo and stopped.

She was wearing sunglasses and pulling an orange suitcase. It was too heavy for her to lift. An unlit cigarette dangled from her lips. She stopped when she saw me and lit the cigarette. She didn't look surprised.

'Well?' she said. 'Are you going to help me with this or not?'

I took the suitcase in my arm and walked behind her as she descended. We went to the reception foyer, past the pool, and the Chinese woman said her taxi would be along, but that she couldn't smoke inside.

'She does know you,' I said.

Lola didn't answer, and we waited out front. I put her case down by her side, and she handed me the cigarette.

'You're going somewhere?' I said.

'Always perceptive,' she said. 'Acutely so.'

I desperately wanted to see her eyes, but she didn't remove her sunglasses.

'I heard you needed help.'

'You heard?'

I nodded dumbly, then said, 'I gave Romeo something for you.'

'I got it.'

'Okay then.'

'Okay?'

'I mean, I'm glad you got it.'

'Sure,' she said. She looked terribly bored by our conversation. She reached out and took the cigarette back from me.

'It's just …' I said awkwardly, 'I wondered.'

'Wondered?' she said, inhaling.

'If … or?'

'What?'

'It's mine?'

'It?'

'The …?' My mouth went dry, and the words caught in my throat. I reached out with one of my hands as if I could pluck the words I needed from the air, but there was nothing there, and my hand returned to my side. The gesture made me feel like I didn't fit my skin. 'And what you've decided …'

She looked into the distance for her cab. 'Decided?'

'If you'll … or not?'

She spat, threw the end of the cigarette onto the ground, and stubbed it out with her stiletto. 'I don't know,' she said. 'I don't know what I'll do. I guess I'll go home and think on it.'

'Okay,' I said.

'Okay then,' she said.

'And you'll let me know.'

'Sure,' she said, the disinterest firm in her face.

'Who and what?'

She let out a weary sigh, and the taxi pulled up. The driver was out before we knew it, pulling her case into the trunk.

'And you'll ...?' I said again as she climbed in.

'I just might,' she said, and the taxi took off. Its exhaust blew a cloud of black smoke so that I had to take a step back, not knowing what she had meant by *I might*, and when I waved the smoke out of my face, and opened my eyes, she and the car were gone. I blinked then, and felt something like those times when we had left the casino together and had lost everything, but that this feeling was more final in a way I found too painful to face.

I drove back to the Garden in a daze. Blanchard was back. He wanted me to burn papers. He said that shredding was not enough. He needed the papers obliterated. Maybe it was to do with tax, the IRS. When I asked, he said the sales he was making were going to have to be cash sales. It all sounded shady. He was working on promises, he said.

'Poof,' he said, raising his hand in the air. 'I want them gone.'

'So shall it be done,' I said.

'Pardon?'

I looked up. The black sack in my hands wafted in the wind.

'What did you say?'

I shrugged.

'Don't mock, Swallow. It's unbecoming.'

I went to the firepit. At first, he brought the papers out by the armful. Bills, contracts, letters, invitations and statements. God knows what else. But there were too many of them, and he eventually resorted to using the wheelbarrow. The papers that blew away, he ordered Miguel to collect. Miguel stumbled and fell. Blanchard looked at the man in consternation, but he made no comment.

All afternoon, the flames rose, and the smoke billowed. When the papers were all deposited and dumped into the pit, I stood stoking it with a long and rusted pole until all that was left was ash. Then, I sat by the edge of the pit and watched the last of the embers fade.

The sun set. Some of the men must have thought the glowing pit was an excuse to kick back and celebrate. They came out, sat next to me with bottles, and drank. I didn't object, and when a bottle was passed to me, I drank.

The men talked quietly. Darkness came, and the stars emerged. After a time, I stood and went back to the barracks. I tried to sleep but couldn't. I walked about the Garden, along its perimeter fence, watching.

Not far in the distance, I heard the howl of a coyote. Next, I heard a band of them cry and whimper. If the men decided to grill, the smells of cooking meat would bring the coyotes closer. Miguel would have no problem shooting one, gutting it and adding its meat to the barbeque. I'd seen him do it before. It was a bloody business, and I'd no desire to see it again.

I took the gun from my pocket and fired a warning shot.

'Coyotes?'

It was Romeo.

He went to the fencing and looked out onto a stretch of scrubland. He lit a cigarette, and in the darkness the brief burn of it brightened his face. He looked troubled. The rough grooves of his features were shadowed, his openness was all but gone. He drew a hand across a scar on his chest.

We stood in silence. Overhead the stars multiplied. When I looked up, they seemed to rush towards me, a thousand suns crowding a keyhole.

'Sometimes, I don't know why I came here,' Romeo
said.

He hadn't been here so long, and it almost sounded
like something I would say.

'Why did you?' I said.

'Blanchard asked me.'

'Blanchard,' I said.

'Yeah, but you know, I could have gone anywhere.'

'So could we all,' I said. The coyotes cried out. 'Maybe
we should never have messed with the ghost.'

He'd dropped his cigarette to the ground and took up
his stance of holding onto the fence again as if he were
exhausted, as if he were desperate to escape. From the
firepit, I could hear one of the men strumming a guitar.

'But we did.'

'And a man is dead.'

I imagined Romeo as me in a decade.

'America ...' he said. 'America promised me more.'

I didn't want to hear his bullshit sob story about
America.

'America?' I said. 'America's a myth. It's the Wild West,
it's a car crash. It's a child with a gun in its hands.'

He was facing me now, in my space.

'Why didn't you tell me about Lola?' I said.

'You fuckin' knew.'

'Oh yeah?'

I took my first punch. He countered with a jab which
wasn't strong, but it was accurate. He bloodied my nose.
I wiped the blood away and spat. I was stronger, but he
was faster.

'You don't care,' he said.

I caught him on the ear, he went for the body. Sweat
and spit and blood was the order of the fight.

He spat, 'Or didn't care.'

I flailed, kicked. He caught me, threw me to the ground.

'You don't know that,' I said.

I wiped my mouth, the metallic taste of blood.

'I don't want to fuck you up,' he said.

I got to my feet, but he floored me with a left hook.

I managed to take him in a headlock, and it ended in a tussle, an awkward embrace. He stepped back, lowered his hands.

I took that as his concession, held out my hand, and he bumped it with his fist. We wiped ourselves down and walked back to the fire.

We drank. And when we drank, nothing mattered. The man with the guitar played a slow ballad. Then someone else sang the saddest song I'd ever heard.

'I made sure she got the money,' he said, without looking up.

I wanted to say thank you, but I couldn't bring myself to say those words – however small and inconsequential they may have been. I was too afraid of what else they may have admitted.

'You're in love with her?' he said.

'Who? Lola?'

'No, Meribel.'

'You think?'

Dawn broke, and Romeo and I made our way back to the barracks. In the distance, there was a cloud of smoke, and then an orange glow. Fields of sugar cane were on fire again. We walked, found ourselves somehow arm in arm.

'I don't think,' he said. 'I know.'

I laughed, felt delirious from the fight, the drink, the truth.

'But,' he added. 'What are you going to do about it?'

I thought about his question, and then looked at the beautiful glow in the sky, burning, deathly, like doomsday, and then Romeo was singing, and for some reason, I felt tears on my cheek. No, it was a shower, I told him, not even that, just a drop of rain.

The next morning, black snow. I woke to ash and soot falling from the sky. Smoke and haze-drift followed. I had an ill feeling of guilt in my gut. I drank a glass of water, and then another, but no amount of water could wash away the despair. I reached beneath my bed for a bottle. The whiskey burned my throat. It made my body shudder.

I'd promised myself many times before that I wouldn't drink in the morning, but it was happening more and more. I put it down to Harper's death, and to what had happened to Meribel. I told myself I needed something to steady my nerves and stop my thoughts from racing. Slowly, the tremor in my hands began to calm. Romeo was outside working. Gunter was by his side. I knew something was not right with me. Blanchard had left and come back again.

'We're close,' he said that morning.

'Close?'

'A buyer.'

'That's great.

'This close.' He held his finger and thumb up so they almost touched. 'A South East Asian consortium.'

I nodded. Then, he and Meribel took coffee on the veranda. They said little to one another. He fed Gunter treats. Finally, Blanchard stood up and walked inside. Meribel took out a fan. She redirected her gaze in my direction. I went back to work.

That night, the Beast came. It was a normal night. As normal as they get, I guess. It was after dinner. The few men that were left were settling in for a night of stories, phone calls, cards and dominoes. A cruiser, its lights flashing, sped up the driveway. No sirens. Two officers got out and went to the house. The reason they came was not a site visit, but a shooting at a nightclub. Nine people had been killed. The news reported the tragedy, but no one had much to say at the barracks. The men who worked here carried on. For them, it was business as usual.

Blanchard was not happy, but not because of the loss of life. He was unhappy because there was a greater presence of cops on the streets, and that meant the Beast coming to the Garden. They snooped, made their way through the barracks, and asked questions about workers and their whereabouts, about all sorts of things Blanchard didn't want to talk about.

They knew many of us were undocumented, that our lives were in the balance, that without the right paperwork we didn't on one level even exist. We were invisible to society, but we were the ones who did the dirty work.

Blanchard spoke to them. After ten minutes or so, one of the officers handed Blanchard a card. They left. Blanchard looked about him. I don't know if he saw me watching. What did it matter? Whether I or the men had watched or not, we knew what was happening. We knew the Beast had been and gone. When you're like us, you don't have to see them with your own eyes. You can sense them, you feel them in the vicinity, approaching. After they'd gone, Blanchard stood on the deck, surveying the Garden. I was waiting for him to issue an order, to question or reprimand us, but he didn't. He did none of those things.

Instead, he came to me. 'It's bad timing,' he said.

I asked him why he had let the Beast in, and he said, 'If we hadn't, they would have come with a warrant.'

The following morning, I woke before anyone. I took the truck and drove. It was a long time before I realised what I was doing or where I was. I stopped on the side of the road as the sun was rising. My mouth was dry. I rubbed my eyes. The Keys before me were beautiful.

In the distance was scrubland and the glades. Here, around me, water, green and fathomless. No traffic. Nothing for miles. Lola and I had been here, or somewhere like it. I could see the photograph I once had of that trip, but I couldn't remember the day, not fully. The memory was all but gone, no matter how much I tried to recall it, all but the navy sweater she wore, and the way her hair was tied back, and her smile; I still remembered that.

We must have been happy. That's my explanation. The image sufficed, until the memory faded, and the photograph was lost. There was a time we could have made a go of it, but that time was gone. I knew now my heart belonged to another. I thought about driving west along the Gulf Coast. I could do it. And I did for a time, drive on, for miles without thinking, letting the road unroll before me. Then I stopped again for gas. I could make the state line by nightfall, I thought – leave it all behind. But just as quickly, as soon as I realised what I was doing, the energy drained from my body. A series of unconscious arguments went on within me. Go, stay. All of it at some stage rehearsed in my dreams, and in the years that had passed me by. And now the realisation that I was where I was for a reason. I had found a place to be. Meribel, the ghost, the Garden, they were meant for me. I turned around and drove, with an urgent longing, the same road home.

Back at the Garden, it was dark. I made my way to the barracks; nobody said anything to me. By all appearances, it was as if I hadn't even left, as if my wavering hadn't mattered. But my soul was an invincible summer, and the thought pulsed through me like a second heartbeat: something's got to give; something's got to change.

I went to the barracks. The few men left lay about. Some played cards. There was nothing different about the look of the scene. And I wasn't sure whether I could trust my intuition. I couldn't even tell if I was thinking straight. What I did notice was a perceptible displacement in the atmosphere. It could simply have been me, I was the men's supervisor after all, but I thought it was something else: a wariness, a shifting in the air. Then I saw Romeo leave the main house. He strode towards the barracks, and I walked outside to meet him.

'Where've you been?' he said quietly.

Before I had a chance to answer he said, 'Something's happened.'

'What?'

He looked me dead in the eye, and said, 'Miguel's been shot.'

'No?'

'He's hanging on.'

'What happened? Was it Logan?'

Romeo nodded. 'I guess Miguel owed him money for drugs, and I think the con with the Miccosukee didn't help.'

Romeo paced back and forth, then the door to the main house opened. It was Blanchard.

I said, 'We need to get him to a hospital.'

But I couldn't bring him, not after what had happened with Meribel. This time, I knew if I went it would put us all at risk.

'He's lost too much blood,' Romeo said.

'He could die then,' I said.

Blanchard took out a cigar from his jacket. He cut the end of it off with a knife and said, 'And if he docs, you'll dig another grave.'

This man who I had trusted once, he had changed so much. The obsession with the ghost orchid had eaten away at his decency; he had become something almost unrecognisable to me. 'Then I'll bring him,' I said.

'You're not going anywhere,' Blanchard answered. 'We need you here.'

'Then Meribel can bring him.'

'No,' he said.

Romeo and I went to the lab. Miguel was lying on a mattress surrounded by the cuttings and instruments of our trade. His eyes flickered in the half-light.

I knelt, then ripped open his shirt, and wiped away the blood.

'Get me a knife,' I said.

Miguel groaned.

Romeo bent over him and said, 'Don't worry amigo, it won't hurt.'

Miguel let out a nervous laugh, and I wiped the sweat from his brow.

'Hombre,' he said.

'Quiet, you old fool.'

I took a flask of whiskey from his pocket and put it to his lips.

He drank, then coughed, 'Will I die?'

I took Romeo's knife, shook my head in answer to his question, doused the knife in whiskey and dug open the wound. Miguel groaned desperately. I'd done this once before in Guatemala for a local boy who'd been shot by one of my men. The boy had died.

'Stop him from howling,' Romeo said.

I reached out and found a small piece of wood.

'Bite on this.'

He sank his teeth into the wood, his eyes wide and wild with fear and pain. Then I dipped the knife further into the wound.

He howled. I made a mess, but I found the bullet and took it out. Romeo sponged Miguel's sweating body, and I held the bullet up to the light of the moon, which streamed through the lab window, then sealed the wound with a piece of ripped shirt.

Miguel struggled to take the medal of our Lady about his neck and kiss it.

'Gracias,' he said.

His eyes were sunken into his head. He closed them and drifted in and out of consciousness. Then he coughed, sat up and spat blood into the dirt. He lay back down.

'Where's the whiskey?' Romeo said.

I gave it to him, and he drank and crossed himself. There was a low hum from the equipment around us. The orchid looked tiny, forlorn – hardly worth all this.

'You brought him in here?' I said.

'Yes.'

'And Logan?

'I guess he wanted payback, and when he didn't get it he thought he'd take the ghost.'

'But he didn't …'

Romeo shook his head. 'We scared him off before he could.'

But not before Miguel had been shot. 'Fuck,' I said. I put my hand on Miguel's forehead. It was cold. 'It's going to be okay,' I said.

Romeo handed me a cigarette. It wasn't long before a line of ants had found their way to the pool of blood by Miguel's side. Romeo blew smoke rings, and the ants drank the blood greedily.

Blanchard came to the lab then. 'He's not going to make it,' I said.

He and Romeo both knew I needn't have said those words. There was the charade of watching him, but it also felt like we were waiting for Miguel to take his last breath.

Later, we brought him towards the firepit. The men were feeding him tequila now. He was delirious.

'We need to take him to the hospital,' I said.

Romeo was poking at the fire with a stick.

He said, 'You know we can't do that, Swallow.'

He was right. And if I'd called the Beast it would mean investigations and arrests. We'd all go down. Even Meribel would be implicated as an accomplice.

'He'll die,' I said.

Romeo swabbed Miguel's wound. 'He's going to bleed until there is no more blood in him,' he said sadly, shaking his head. He held up a cloth in his hand, dirty with blood, and squeezed it. The blood dripped onto the ground. This time, there was no pool, or line of ants. This time, the earth soaked up every drop.

That night, when Miguel had exhaled his last breath, we placed his body in the crudely dug cavity as carefully as we could. But the grave wasn't big enough.

I looked to Romeo.

'Jacaranda roots,' he said.

He was right. The soil was dense with the gnarled and tangled roots of that tree. I tried anyway, dug in vain until the spade's handle snapped in my hands.

'Help me,' I said, kneeling. Romeo joined me. 'Here,' I said, taking one of Miguel's legs and bending it. Romeo did the same. 'Careful,' I said, 'or you'll snap it.'

I crossed Miguel's arms to fit him into the hole, and then I sat back. He looked as best he could. Who had ever heard of a grave not fitting? I stood up again, dug my hands into the dirt and threw it onto the body, filling the grave then, one shovelful after another. I promised I would re-dig it and lay him out with some respect. I threw the last of the soil to cover his face; a crumb of dirt fell through his lips. Poor supper, I thought. We were now in hell.

'Pray for us sinners,' I said, 'now and at the hour of our death.'

Romeo bowed his head, and said, 'Amen.'

That night Romeo and I played cards. Blanchard joined us but did not play. He poured us each a glass of whiskey.

'What's the game?' he asked.

'Five card.'

He watched us studiously, as if he cared. Lord knows where his head was at. After we'd played a few hands, Romeo said, 'What if they come back?'

'Why would they do that?' Blanchard said, though the way he said it, you could tell he knew it was a possibility. He stood up then, and said he was going to check on Meribel.

Romeo said, 'You think they'll be back?'

'If they come, we'll be waiting.' I reached to my waistband, flicked my shirt away and touched the gun there.

Blanchard returned. I poured us all another drink.

'To Miguel,' I said. 'One of the best men I knew.'

Romeo and Blanchard raised their glasses.

'A man who died for no good reason,' I said, directing this to Blanchard, but he didn't flinch, just downed his whiskey and shuddered where he sat. Whatever about my anger, I suppose I felt a pang of guilt too, knowing that I might have been able to prevent Miguel's death.

When Romeo offered that it was all fucked up, Blanchard said, 'We'll take turns keeping watch.'

'I'm not sleeping,' I said.

'Okay,' Blanchard said. 'Romeo's right. Logan might just be crazy enough to come back. We need to be on our guard.'

'And the ghost?' Romeo said.

Blanchard lit a cigar, 'It stays in the lab,' he said. 'It's the only way it'll survive. But we need the men.'

'You mean what's left of them,' I said.

After the dismissals and Miguel's death, we were down to just four men. I had no idea if they would stay and put their lives on the line for Blanchard. When I went to the barracks to check, it was empty. Sure, their stuff was still there, but they had taken off. They must have seen what was coming. They'd had enough and made for it. I can't say I blamed them, not one bit. And so we sat and waited. The temperature dropped, and we kept the fire going, throwing on one log after another.

Meribel came out. 'I don't like it,' she said.

'Please go back inside,' Blanchard said, but she ignored him. He stood up, and she just stepped aside, took the bottle from Romeo's hand and drank.

'Let's go in,' he said to her, but she refused, and in a fit of pique, he said 'fine' and left her with us.

Romeo went to the barracks and lay in the hammock. I said I'd mind shop. For a time, it was peaceful. Starlight and orchids. Meribel and I walked through the grounds, then went to the lab to check on the ghost breathing quietly in its special chamber – like a life support system for an alien being. The desperate lengths people will go to for beauty, I thought; how they'll shed blood.

Her hand brushed against mine, and she turned to me. I kissed her, and it felt like we were falling through space.

'Come on,' she said then, and for a moment I didn't know where I was. We made our way across the Garden; somehow it felt like we were at the threshold of something, and that we were about to cross it together. Then all of a sudden I heard the gears of a truck grind on the driveway. I imagined this was it. This was what we'd been waiting for. But where were the soldiers now? Where was the army? All Blanchard had was me, Romeo and Meribel.

'What's that?' she said.

The roar of the engine got closer, then the truck sped up the gravel driveway. It skidded to a halt, and I ran into the open. I called for Romeo. A shot was fired. I took Meribel's hand and squeezed. 'Get inside. Take cover,' I said, and she ran towards the house. Then four men carrying fire-lit torches jumped off the back of the truck and spread out. By the look of them they were a raggle-taggle band of outlaws, a mix of whites and Hispanics, like the men I'd seen once at Deckards. They whooped and hollered, swung their torches.

Two went to the greenhouses, another two to the shade-house. I heard breaking glass and the sound of fire catching. The man who'd been driving climbed out. It was Logan, a bold swagger about him. Then Blanchard emerged from the house and ran to my side.

'Where's Romeo?' he said.

'By the barracks. You still don't want to call the Beast?'

'It's too late.'

Blanchard walked towards the truck and said, 'I'll reason with him.'

Logan approached, a shotgun in his hands. Blanchard went to speak to him, but Logan side-swiped him on the jaw with the gun's butt. Blanchard fell to his knees, stunned.

All around was chaos. The lab was in flames, and the barracks too. I saw Romeo stumble out, smoke in his eyes, wincing and looking about him in horror. Logan walked towards the lab. Gunter ran for him, but Logan shot the dog dead and it fell to the ground with a whimper.

Logan kept on towards the lab while I went to Blanchard's aid, but he pushed me away and scrambled after Logan. I then turned to see Romeo fighting with two of the men.

'Ándale,' he shouted to me, looking for help.

Logan's men went to town, upending the tables where the flowers grew, stomping on them while choking black smoke tunnelled its way through the greenhouses. Windows and pots were smashed, and shade-cloths torn and ripped. It was worse than the hurricane; it felt like the end of the world.

Meribel appeared onto the veranda with a shotgun in her hands. She aimed it at Logan. He looked at her, and she fired into the sky, but it didn't scare him. He kept walking towards the lab, while one of the other men went for the house and Meribel.

I had a choice to make.

Meribel shot at Logan this time, but missed, a shell lodging inside one of the pines with a thunk. One of the men was nearing her, wielding a knife, as she struggled to reload. I went to where he was and struck the back of his head with the pistol. But he didn't go down; he turned instead, and I headbutted him. I heard his nose crunch and break. This time it knocked him down, and he fell to his knees.

The word *pacify* came to me. 'Pacify the enemy' is what we had been told to do at boot camp, so that is what I did. I bent down and straddled the man. I shouted at Meribel to look away. She ran from where we were, and I took the man's ears in my hands and pulled on them with the utmost force, just like I'd been trained to do, and they peeled off the side of his head like the sound of paper ripping.

He howled.

Screaming, burning, gunfire – a little night music.

I threw the two leathery ears into the dirt, and the man hobbled to the truck and started its engine. Then the three other men ran to it and climbed aboard. That is when Logan came into view. I saw the winsome image of the ghost in his mouth. He was tearing at it, chewing it in horrible bloody mouthfuls, swallowing it with globs of blood and sputum.

Romeo went for him, but one of the men on the truck shot and hit him. He fell to his knees, but it didn't look fatal. The truck screeched into action and drove to where he was, two of the men jumping off and hauling Romeo onto the truck. It sped away. I couldn't make out if Logan had found his way onto the truck or not. I looked to Meribel from the front of the house, dismayed, then I ran to the lab. The windows were smashed, the door flung open. The air was fanning the flames from inside. I heard Blanchard ranting and crying out.

The heat from the flames was warping the wood about the door frame, and I struggled to make my way inside. I was met by a wall of heat and was pushed back by it. At first, I couldn't see Blanchard, the smoke was so thick.

The blaze was spreading from the back of the lab with ferocious speed. Then, I heard him cough, and splutter, and from a black cloud of smoke, Blanchard appeared like a dusty dark angel.

'It's gone,' he said, holding the broken ghost chamber in his hands. He picked it up above his head and flung it to the ground, where it smashed into a thousand pieces. 'Gone!'

There was a bloodthirst in his eyes.

'Get out of my way,' he said.

I held my ground.

'What are you doing, Swallow? The ghost is gone. Get the fuck out of my way.'

A swell of anger rose again from deep within me. I hated Blanchard right then, for what he had done to Meribel, for letting Romeo be taken, for keeping me, as I saw it, at the Garden, and for all the unnameable anguishes of our lives. I took the pistol from my belt and aimed it at his heart.

He walked towards me and began to laugh. 'Is that my Smith? Christ, Swallow, give that to me. I can use it on the Indian and get back what's ours.'

'It's not ours,' I said.

I cocked the hammer. The fire closed in. Blanchard coughed. He doubled over, then stood straight. The smoke was in my eyes now, and they stung. I closed them, and it was then that he lunged for me. He grappled and grabbed at my hands. The gun fell from my grip and onto the floor.

We wrestled, dropped to the ground, and I punched him once, then twice in the side of the head, and he laughed, so I punched him harder, this time in the Adam's apple. He gasped, then reached out to choke me. I struck him again with full force and heard my knuckles crack against his cheekbone. He gouged my eyes with his fingers, and they stung, then bled.

We found our way to our feet and fought some more. Blood clouded my vision. I reached for the gun, found it, and dragged myself away. Then I held the gun up, pulled the trigger and fired a shot into his chest. I watched him go down, without a word, not even like a deck of cards, but more like a marionette.

My hand shook. I panicked. What have I done, I wondered. And as quickly, I thought about how I might say he was burned by the fire, or overcome by smoke, and if the gunshot wound was recognised, I could say that it was Logan, or that it had gone off in his own hands.

I walked over to him. He was breathing heavily, and for a split second I felt pity and regret for what I had done. He reached out his hand, and I thought he wanted to say something, some last confession, so I bent down. But he was not trying to confess anything to me.

He put a hand on my blood-stained and fire-singed face and raised a knife, from whence I do not know. Then he brought it down on me with such force that I could feel the darkness enter me like a lightning strike. I struggled to breathe, and just as it all went black, I heard the boom of another gunshot. I felt my blood leave my body in a hot gush, and the last thing I saw before I blacked out was Meribel standing in the doorway with the shotgun in her hands.

There were times when I found myself looking up from the work I was doing and gazing towards the driveway, half expecting to see him. Bag slung over his shoulder, smiling, raising a hand in greeting. There were times when I started with fright, through some trick of the light, when I thought it was actually Romeo, standing there, somehow come back, but it never was. It was someone else, or a shadow cast by the needles of the pine trees, or simply my own mind.

Weeks passed. I recovered from my injuries, though there remained a stiffness in my arm and neck. I took his cigarettes and smoked them one after another in an unending afternoon of cold sunshine. It was only then I noticed that Harper's aspen sculpture of the horse called Tama was gone from my bedside. Romeo hadn't seemed interested in it when I had told him how Harper had made it, yet now it was gone. I can't imagine it was he who had taken it; more likely it was Catfish, hiding it in his carry-all as a souvenir of the place before he left.

Days later, I swept beneath his bed and took the mattress outside and burned it like it was my own private ritual, my own private grief I was attending to. And so it was, I guess. Then one day, a man arrived. He was covered in a film of dust. He walked slowly, one careful step after another. There was something resigned but determined about him, something which said that, though he didn't mean trouble, he did mean business. As he approached, I caught his eye, and he made sure that his never left mine. Before his lips even parted, I knew what he was going to say, but before he did, I offered him a cup of water. He took it without a word and drank it down. He wiped his lips with the back of his hand and said the name I had been waiting for.

'Romeo.'

I let the name catch on the breeze and disperse like smoke, and in the undergrowth, I heard a scrub jay weep.

'He's gone,' I said.

'Where to?'

'I don't know.'

The man was unnerved, but not surprised. He looked like he'd been travelling for a long time, traveling his whole life, as if it was his mission to traipse, to wander, and search.

'His work here is done?' he said cryptically.

'I guess.'

'And you're Swallow?'

'I am.'

He offered me a cigarette. I took one, and we smoked without talking.

'I need to find him,' he said finally.

He smiled, then took the cap from his head and ran a hand through his thinning hair. He took a deep breath.

'You were his friend. He spoke of you.'

'He did?'

The man nodded, his lungs full of smoke. I thought of Romeo's carry-all, the bag beneath his bed. I thought about telling the man about it, giving it to him.

'Follow me,' I said.

I walked towards the barracks.

'Are you family?'

At first, the man didn't answer. I thought maybe he hadn't heard me. When we got to the barracks' door, he said, 'I'm Romeo's father.'

He said it with such sadness, I couldn't bring myself to show him inside. I stopped at the entrance and turned.

'He liked it here.'

I said, 'Yes, he did.'

'He liked it very much. He said you took good care of him.'

'He said that?'

'Yes.'

I thought about how Romeo had told me his parents had been killed, and of what Catfish had said. It was hard to make sense of the world.

'Do you think …?' his voice trailed off. 'Do you think he is still alive?'

The man smiled nervously. It was a hideous smile, as though his teeth hadn't been lost by decay, but had been removed by force, knocked out by fist, or blunt trauma. He stood there forlornly, as if his face had never forgiven him.

I told him some of what had happened, that the night we were raided Romeo had disappeared.

'And the boss? Blanchard?'

'Gone too,' I said.

Behind me was the smell of rotting meat. *Satyrium pumilum* was in bloom, its black tongue hanging out, its tiny yellow flowers attracting flies. A South African orchid, it was leafy and hard-wearing. We were starting to rebuild.

When it came time to say goodbye, the man took my hand in his. I thought he might weep, but he didn't. And all that sleepless night, the putrid stench of the

African orchid stayed with me. By dawn I had washed and scrubbed my skin raw, but still, it seemed, the smell clung to me, and the rising sun, I knew, would only make it worse.

Gradually, the Garden changed. My own bed in the barracks was taken by another. A young man, a boy really, from Peru. He spoke very little English, but he worked hard. He was watchful, and resourceful. His name was Juan. In some ways, he reminded me of Romeo.

And there was something about how, as night approached, a space within me opened – an emptiness, a void that asked to be filled. Those days, I filled it with work. I tended to the Garden. I nurtured and encouraged each seed, each sapling, and watched one season turn into another. With Black Fox, we'd come to an arrangement; it was to stay out of each other's way, as I understood it.

I had met him at a Walmart, his trolley full with clothes and soda and other things I couldn't make out. His head was bowed, and he wore a pair of worn slippers. At first, he didn't see me, but I stopped, and when he looked up, he acknowledged me.

'Hello,' he said.

'I've meant to call by,' I told him.

He nodded his head and puckered his lower lip. 'I'm retired now,' he said.

'I thought maybe you might like to …'

He stared at me without a word. 'What happened, Swallow? What happened that night?'

Was I going to tell him, in the condiment aisle, what I thought had happened? No, I was not. I asked him where Logan was, and Romeo. He went to speak, but thought twice of it, and when he turned away, I let go of my trolley and took a hold of his arm.

'Where's Romeo?'

'I don't know,' he said.

He took a step back, looked me in the eye and repeated the words, 'I don't know.'

Romeo – was he the casualty of another man's greed, or a victim of chance, a poor player in a drama not of his making? I'm not sure I'll ever know, and there didn't seem much else to do but to accept what Black Fox had said. We shook hands, and I watched him push his trolley and shuffle down the aisle.

The weeks passed. Black Fox came by with the statue of John Horse that Harper had once made. 'Thought you might like this,' he said. I took it and thanked him before he left. Neither of us mentioned Logan or Romeo, but there was talk of a new crop at the Garden. And as time passed, Meribel helped me into Blanchard's suits. We didn't throw all my old clothes out. I still had work to do. Some nights, Meribel and I drove downtown to the maze of bridges where the homeless lived. We handed out food but the men we had once met there were all gone. In America, they're called transients. Where I was from, they're called blow-ins, which to me made more sense. After all, many of the plants I saw about me from one day to the next had found their way here on the breath of a breeze, and tried as best they could to take root and grow, though most did not make it.

As we entered into a new season, we decided not to take on any new men. Besides, slowly, they were leaving us. We were alright with that. We didn't fire anyone. They just left, as if they realised there was no future for them here. Whereas I felt differently. Spring was on its way, and with it a sense of – dare I say it, after all the bloodshed – hope.

At night, I sat on the veranda and brooded on what had brought me here. I remembered Harper. I wore his dog tags. I remembered Miguel, Catfish, and thought too of Romeo's journey from Honduras to Belize, and from there to the Garden. I thought about how he had tended the ghost for Blanchard, a man who had been blinded by the need to take something which did not belong to him, nor to any of us for that matter. Call it theft, or a form of trespass. Call it whatever you want. It didn't matter. We had transgressed, and the glades in the distance knew it. God, whatever or whoever he was, knew it, and my dear departed brother knew it too. I had told Lola we would be saved; what I should have said to her, wherever she was, was that we would be judged, but not in this lifetime.

ACKNOWLEDGEMENTS

Thank you to Melanie Hobson, friend, novelist and Florida resident who gave a first read to an early draft and helped make *The Garden* a stronger book. We met many years ago in Miami where I also met novelist Michelle Richmond, who always has my back, and believed in this book. Thank you. David Morgan O'Connor's support was constant, his reading and insights invaluable. Thank you to novelist Mia Gallagher who has always inspired, and who spoke words of wisdom and reassurance when I needed them.

Thank you to colleagues in the School of English at UCD, especially Professors Danielle Clarke and John Brannigan, and to my Creative Writing colleagues, Anne Enright, Declan Hughes, Sarah Moss, Ian Davidson, and Paula McGrath for the good cheer throughout. And thank you to Sarah Bannan for support, recommendations, and for going above and beyond. Thank you John Balaban whom I first met in Miami and who was my teacher, and mentor. And to Christian Nagle, and Claire Haft who both read early drafts and gave me excellent advice.

Thank you to the whole team at New Island, an independent publisher I have admired for many years, especially to Commissioning Editor Aoife K. Walsh, and Assistant Editor Stephen Reid, whose endless patience and professional scrutiny of *The Garden* made it a better novel. Thank you to the Arts Council of Ireland for a Literature Bursary in 2020 which helped with the completion of this novel.

And final thanks and love to my wife Aoife for reading drafts and supporting me during the time it took to complete *The Garden* and for keeping the home-ship afloat.